LUCY, UNCENSORED

MEL HAMMOND &
TEGHAN HAMMOND

ALFRED A. KNOPF
NEW YORK

THIS IS A BORZOI BOOK PUBLISHED BY ALFRED A. KNOPF.

Visit us on the Web! GetUnderlined.com

Educators and librarians, for a variety of teaching tools,
visit us at RHTeachersLibrarians.com

Library of Congress Cataloging-in-Publication Data is available upon request.
ISBN 978-0-593-81405-5 (trade) — ISBN 978-0-593-81406-2 (lib. bdg.) —
ISBN 978-0-593-81407-9 (ebook)

The text of this book is set in 11-point Adobe Garamond Pro.

Editor: Marisa DiNovis
Interior Designer: Megan Shortt
Jacket Designer: Angela Carlino
Production Editor: Melinda Ackell
Managing Editor: Jake Eldred
Production Manager: Natalia Dextre

Printed in the United States of America
10 9 8 7 6 5 4 3 2 1
First Edition

I dedicate this book to my parents
and amazing co-author sister.

—T

Samesies. Love ya, Teeg.

—M

1

I'VE ONLY BEEN PRACTICING THIS whole "presenting as a girl" thing for a year, but I'm killing it with today's outfit: black turtleneck, white power blazer, high-waisted slacks, hoop earrings. Plus the sharpest, most symmetrical cat-eye liner you ever saw. It only took about a hundred tries and three YouTube tutorials.

Callie, on the other hand, still has a drool mark on the left side of her chin, and so help me goddess if she's about to pull a stained hoodie over her button-down.

"You can't wear that, Cal." I lick my thumb and wipe the crust from her chin. "There's literally a ketchup stain on the boob."

She pouts and bats her eyelashes. "But I need the comfort of its familiar embrace to carry me through this momentous day." Her voice is scratchy. She probably didn't wake up until I texted her that Dad and I were on the way. I've been up for hours, even though Callie and I stayed up until two, texting about how the day would go.

"Girls?" Asha, Callie's stepmom, calls from downstairs. "Almost ready?"

Callie's fluffy five-pound Chihuahua emerges from a pile of crumpled clothes on the chair. "What do you think, Meatball?" I ask, petting him on the forehead. He opens his mouth in a huge yawn. "See? He says, 'Where's that new cardigan we picked out?'" We hit the thrift shop last weekend—the best place to stock up on new, cheap clothes for a baby trans like me. And great for Callie, too, who's already spent her September paycheck on an exotic snack subscription box and color-changing LED strips, which light up her room like a year-round Christmas tree.

Callie groans and peels a beige cardigan off the iguana cage in the corner. Queen Elizardbeth—who, I must specify, is five feet long, nose to tail—gazes back at her sympathetically.

"I look frumpy in this," Callie says, but puts it on.

I don't tell her that the sweater smells like the romaine lettuce rotting under Liza's heat lamp. "You look great," I say. "Let's go."

"Girls?" Asha shouts. "We're late!"

"Hip bump power up!" Callie says.

We raise our arms and bump our hips together three times—the "handshake" we invented in middle school and are still doing as honest-to-goddess legal adults. Then Callie sticks her ass at me and wiggles it.

"You idiot." I smack her booty and we head toward the car.

The ride to Central University takes a little under an hour, since Dad's driving. Mom wanted to join, but the pillow pulled

2

over her head this morning told me she wasn't up for a day of walking around campus. Her cancer's in remission, but her fatigue isn't.

Asha sits up front drinking a baby-shit-green breakfast smoothie, and Callie and I slouch in the back scrolling through our College Dreams Pinterest board. Since I last checked, Callie has added three new images of a make-your-own-waffle bar that allegedly exists in one of the dining halls, plus some photo mural ideas for our dorm room. (We have a roommate pact, obviously. An added perk of me being out as a girl.) I added a tip sheet for students applying to the Hughes drama program. Number one: Nail your audition. Number two: Slam dunk your application. Number three: If you should be so lucky as to land an interview, schmooze those fools to the moon and back.

Luckily, today is just a tour, so we aren't being evaluated. Officially. But you better believe I'm going to be *on*. Just in case.

By the time I wrangle my body out of Dad's SUV, my legs are stiff as uncooked pasta. I check my makeup in the window, ignoring Dad's side-eye. Trust me, he's come a long way from the shouting tornado he turned into on the nights I came out—first as gay and then, after I figured my shit out, as trans. But he still acts shifty when I dress extra girly or dare to swallow my hormones in his presence.

"This is it, Lucy!" Callie yells. Callie jumps straight into the *Footloose* dance we used as an audition piece for our freshman-year musical, and I hop in next to her. It's no surprise that we worked crew for that show.

"The Dream's almost here," she says, arms flailing, toes pointing. "We're college kids now."

"Or are we college *adults*?" I ask, since we both turned eighteen over the summer.

"You're college *kids* in eleven months," Dad says, locking the car. "Don't get carried away."

Asha takes a brush from her purse and pulls it through Callie's shoulder-length dirty-blond hair. "Honestly, Callie, on tour day?" The contrast between Callie and her stepmom is stark—Asha is Indian American with brown skin and silky black hair, and she doesn't start the day without her green smoothie and eight-step skin care routine. Callie is white, pays no mind to her acne, and doesn't leave bed before eleven a.m. if she can help it.

"It's not like it's the interview." Callie pulls away and adds some of the signature muss back to her hairstyle.

If we get through the first round of the Hughes selection process, they'll call us back for a formal interview with the board of directors and some of the theater professors. The Hughes program is super good but super competitive, especially for a state school. And that means a whole extra application process, with essays, fees, and the perfect excuse to dress up like the badass professional lady I truly am. Maybe next time I'll brave the formidable pencil skirt.

"Well, you ready—?" Dad starts to say my deadname and inelegantly slips into "Lllllucy?" He draws it out as if it's an unfamiliar word he picked from the dictionary.

I can't tell if he's still messing up by accident or if he truly has not climbed aboard the transgender train so long after departure. Either way, best to take care of this issue now. "If you pronounce my name like that, everyone will think you're some creepy stranger instead of my dad." I'm not the person who can straight-up call somebody out—that's more Callie's style—but the joke should keep him in line. Hopefully.

"Sorry, kid," he tells me. "I'm trying." He usually tries harder when Mom's around.

"Let me get a picture, girls," Asha says, ushering Callie and me in front of the Central University sign. "Beautiful, Lucy. I love the blazer."

"Thanks. Thrift shop." Asha always makes a point to call Callie and me *girls* and squeeze my name into casual conversation as often as possible, without it being awkward. Did I mention I love Asha?

A chilly October fog blankets the ground, which makes the campus seem even bigger than it is—like it's a vast city that goes on forever. As we step into the cloud world, Callie takes under-the-chin selfies in front of everything. A bench with an abandoned soda cup. A tree exploding with orange leaves. A pedestal with a bearded man's statue head on top.

Asha sighs. "I don't know why you insist on looking ridiculous in every picture you take."

"Because I'm a wrinkly-necked ghost roaming my ghost kingdom," Callie replies, gesturing to the fog. She juts her chin down to create more neck folds. "Plus, beauty is a social construct. Get in this one, Luce."

She pulls my body into hers, and we pose in front of a half-eaten sandwich abandoned on a railing. I extend my head away from my neck and smile with my eyes. I've practiced this pose in the mirror, not quite as ready as Callie is to defy conventional beauty standards.

The campus is empty, which gives the fog an eerie, malicious feeling. Everyone must be sleeping in after crazy all-night parties. The kind of parties Callie and I have dreamed about for years—drinking cheap booze out of red Solo cups, dancing atrociously with other drama nerds, smoking pot on the roof of the theater at two a.m. and then making chili cheese fries in the dorm microwave while we sing along to cast recordings of underappreciated Broadway shows.

Eventually we make it to the quad, where we're supposed to meet our tour guide. The mist hangs low on the grassy area, and the trees rise up like towers that disappear into the sky. Finally, we spot some humans through the haze, bundled in jackets and knit caps. I probably should've added an outer layer to my getup, but covering up this blazer would be a punishable crime.

I imagine myself from the other students' perspectives: a tall girl with pale skin and a dark brown, grown-out pixie cut, emerging from the fog like a mysterious forest nymph. I lighten my stride to look a little more graceful. To them, I could be anyone.

"Callie Katz and Lucy Myers?" the tour guide chirps. He's a clean-cut college kid with a clipboard in his hand. We nod. "Looks like we've got everyone."

Dad gives me a thumbs-up. "Nice. They got your name right," he says under his breath. "I was afraid they'd have you listed as—" But I wallop him with my eyeballs. The tour hasn't even started yet and he's already poking at my self-esteem balloon with a dead-naming needle.

Thankfully, I signed up for the tour with my real name. My

application will be a different story, though, since I'll have to send my transcript and Social Security number and who knows what else. Yes, I'm saving for a name change. My parents don't see the point, since everyone already calls me Lucy. For Dad, coughing up the cash for my hormone copays every month is more than enough financial allyship.

My balloon deflates a little more when I spot two guys from our high school across the tour group. Lewis and Ben—the human equivalents of stale toast. They're part of the susurrus of school life: the never-face-to-face deadnaming, misgendering, and general ignorance that float around me every day. College was supposed to be my bug-fixing update for that issue. But obviously we're going to run into high school classmates at a Pennsylvania state school an hour from home. Duh.

Callie meets my gaze and rolls her eyes. "Ignore those poop quesadillas," she whispers.

I hold my head a little higher and put all my senses on red alert: one ear on Dad and one eye on Lewis and Ben. (Are they snickering at me or did the tour guide crack a joke?)

Our first stop is the Elmo Henderson Memorial Student Center and Dining Hall. A few dozen students sit around drinking coffee and typing on laptops. While the tour group gathers in the lobby, Callie strides straight to the serving stations to suss out the waffle bar situation.

"Not here," she says when she gets back. "Must be in a different dining hall."

"We'll find it," I tell her.

"What I *can* say is that college cuisine appears to be much more sophisticated than high school food."

"Waffle bars are sophisticated?"

"Yes! They're rumored to include fruit."

"Next to the Reese's Pieces, of course."

"Naturally. You'll also find this institution offers not chicken nuggets but rather delicate poultry morsels," Callie says in the snooty British accent she's been working on. "You must eat them with fork and knife. And you shan't be excused from the table until you've sampled the leavened flatbread with herbed tomato and aged milk garnish." Pizza, I suppose.

She's trying to egg me on, but all I can manage is a dry laugh. I'm too distracted to really get into it. Lewis stares at me as Callie and I rejoin everyone. He elbows Ben, who gives me a look that's hard to interpret. Amused, maybe? Amusing definitely isn't what I was going for when I got dressed this morning. I love my outfit, but I probably would've toned it down if I'd realized people from school would be here. I've kept my Monday-through-Friday outfits on the androgynous side to make life easier. I herd Callie to the edge of the group, keeping as many bodies as possible between us and the guys.

Before long, we enter the lobby of the Hughes Auditorium. Callie gasps as if we've just infiltrated an ancient Egyptian pyramid. Framed playbills paper one wall, and colorful sculptures hang from the ceiling. The guide doesn't have to tell us that the school's theater department lives right here. I feel it intrinsically, and Callie's ecstatic drama-nerd face tells me she hears the same Hallelujah choir bursting into song.

"Can you remind me of the different drama concentrations?"

Callie asks, as if she hasn't already memorized the theater-major page on Central's website.

While the guide answers, my ears yank me around to face Dad, who's talking softly with another parent. "Yeah, she's been in drama club all through high school." I smile at the woman, who smiles back. So far so good, but damn, Dad is putting me on edge.

"You said there's a *directing* concentration?" Callie says, urging me with her eyebrows to get excited. "That's so cool."

I smile to reassure her that I'm enjoying the tour. For years, our Dream has been to go to the same college together. *This* college. *This* theater program. But running surveillance on Lewis and Ben, who I swear keep staring at me, wasn't on our College Dreams board.

"Do students, uh, get the chance to run their own shows?" I force myself to ask.

Throughout high school, I've waffled between acting, crew, stage managing, and directing. I loved all of it (though audiences could do without my singing), but something about watching a piece come to life from the metaphorical director's chair takes me to the next level. It's like I can take a vision directly from my head and project it onto the stage. And bossing people around is *the best*. Most people don't expect bossiness from me, just because I'm quiet. But directing is a great way for a quiet person to get folks to listen, because, you know, they have to.

"Absolutely," the guide says. "That's one of the great things about the Hughes program—each and every student in the directing concentration gets to direct a show as part of their senior thesis."

One show? Senior year? A sense of not-quite-rightness settles on my shoulders like a scratchy blanket. I thought I'd get to start next year. But I guess in a big program like Hughes, there's only so much stage time to go around.

As we leave the auditorium, a girl walks beside us. "Are you applying for Hughes, too?" She straightens the hair tie at the end of her thick, black braid. Damn. I want that hair.

I run my fingers through my own not-yet-shoulder-length hair, urging it to grow faster. "Yeah, both of us," I say, offering Callie another I'm-invested-in-this-tour smile.

"Cool! I'm doing my audition piece next month." She crosses her fingers. "Acting concentration."

"Me too!" Callie explodes. "We're doing our audition together," she says, wrapping me in a shoulder hug. "It's our senior showcase, which we're codirecting. And costarring in. Oh, and we wrote the script for it together, too."

"I love it!" New Girl declares. "That's really impressive."

Callie nods. "I hesitate to use the term *dream team* in case someone mistakes us for basketball stars, but there's really no better way to describe it." She hip bumps me, and I muster the energy to bump back.

"What other shows have you done?" the girl asks.

"We were both puppeteers in *Pinocchio* our first year," Callie says. "Then we worked crew for *Into the Woods*. Our big breaks came sophomore year, though. I was Ophelia in *Hamlet*."

New Girl nods and looks to me, waiting to hear who I played. I clear my throat. "I, uh, played Hamlet," I mumble. Plenty of women perform men's roles in Shakespeare plays, especially in high

10

school theater. But no one *knew* I was a woman at the time, so bringing it up still makes me shudder.

The girl raises her eyebrows, impressed. "Hamlet? Wow. The theater guys at my school would throw a fit if an underclassman got cast in a role like that. Especially a girl."

It would be generous to call the sound that comes from my mouth a word.

New Girl looks between me and Callie, probably confused about why my forehead has burst into a cold sweat. Finally her eyes snap to my face, my chest, my shoulders, my hips. She's calculating my identity before I've even had a chance to tell her my name. She settles back on my face. *Oh, you're trans,* her eyes say. Then she smiles and nods, too eagerly.

"I need to use the bathroom," I say, feeling like I've just taken a kick to the spleen. I take long, fast steps to get away. Good thing I didn't go with the power heels after all—my flats are mercifully quiet on the shiny tile floor.

"I'm so sorry that happened," Callie whisper-shouts, running to catch up with me.

"It's okay," I say, striding ahead at full speed. "My theatrical career isn't a secret."

"I shouldn't have brought up *Hamlet.*"

I try to put my words in the right order. *Why did such a small comment send me spiraling into a shit-filled swimming pool of anxiety?*

"I'm super-duper sorry, times infinity, with a pile of waffles and whipped cream on top. And a cherry," Callie says.

"You did nothing wrong, Cal." I stop walking because, despite my purposeful steps, I have no idea where the bathrooms are. "It's just—" I swallow, embarrassed at how much the conversation affected me. "The first thing that girl knows about me is that I'm trans. I didn't even get to introduce myself."

"That's shitty," Callie says. "From now on, let's just focus on the showcase when we talk to people."

As if on cue, Lewis and Ben appear behind us, apparently looking for the bathroom, too. *Or are they following me?* A shiver runs down my spine. They're both wearing red-and-gold sweatshirts with Central's mascot, Leo the Lion. Their haircuts are mirror images of one another—short on the sides and swooping up douchily in the front.

"Men's room is this way," Ben says. He heads toward the sign for the men's bathroom, which is around the corner.

Lewis elbows him but holds back a smile. "Shut up, dude," he says. Then to me, "He's just kidding around."

I press my nails into my palms, and my skin heats up like a radiator. Bathrooms are a touchy subject for me, especially after our school suggested that I use the toilet in the nurse's office to avoid "making other students uncomfortable." I declined their suggestion and pretty much just avoid drinking water all day.

"What the *fuck*?" Callie spits. She marches toward Ben, fuming. "I think you shitheads might be in the wrong building. This is a space for intelligent adults. The childcare center is across campus."

Ben holds up his hands in surrender. "My bad, I forgot," he says. But the smirk doesn't leave his face.

In the bathroom, we wrap our arms around each other.

"I'm so sorry that happened," Callie says. "I'm going to report them."

To who? I want to ask but don't. I'm too tired. Lewis and Ben will still get accepted to this school, along with half the college-bound kids in our class. My fresh start is turning into more of a three-month-old-rotting-banana start.

"Thanks for standing up for me" is all I manage to say.

Dad texts that the group has moved to the student center next door, and we rejoin them. The guide is standing in front of a wall covered floor to ceiling with photos of students. "We have over three hundred student organizations," he says. "We encourage students to get involved in campus life outside of classes. And if you don't see your perfect club, you can start your own! All students can carve out a space for themselves here at Central University."

He says it like he means it. And maybe it's true for cisgender people who aren't carrying around a thousand pounds of baggage from elementary, middle, and high school. But I'm beginning to think it's going to take a lot more than starting a club for this school to feel like the right fit.

Callie squeezes my hand. I know she's saying, *I'm sorry for what happened* and *I'm excited to be here* at the same time.

I squeeze back. And she has no idea I'm saying, *This tour fucking sucked.*

2

THE MONDAY AFTER THE CENTRAL
tour, Callie and I are snuggled into our nest of
jackets, backpacks, and snacks in the front row of
our high school auditorium. Mr. Walker calls our
space the Groundling Gallery, named after the rowdy
spectators of Shakespeare's plays, because we laugh too
loud, curse a lot, and have been known to throw rotten
food at the actors. (It only happened once, and it was just
stale gummy worms.)

Mr. Walker paces back and forth at the foot of the stage, deep
in a lecture about Aristotle, something something, realm of perfect ideas reflected in art. Dramatic theory isn't my favorite, but
Mr. Walker makes it interesting for those of us who've stuck with
theater long enough to reach senior seminar. Today he's wearing a
baby-blue paisley button-down with black slacks. He's one of the
few Black teachers at our high school and one of even fewer with
any style. We're obsessed with him.

"All right," Mr. Walker says, sweeping his dreadlocks out of his face. "Let's end a bit early and get to work on those showcase pieces." He turns to Callie and me, and the dreads fall right back over his eyes. "We're just a month and a half out from opening night. Count the days on your calendars, folks. It'll go by fast."

I stare at my fuchsia Converses and make a conscious decision to *not* count the days. I'm not emotionally prepared to carry that burden.

"*Othello,* you have the stage first," Mr. Walker says, nodding to Carlos and Andre. They're the other senior pair directing a showcase. "*Tempest* folks, run lines in the shop. I'll come grab you when the stage is free." He means us, though we've renamed our show *The Storm.* And I swear, Callie and I wrote our *Tempest* retelling months before Carlos and Andre had even read *Othello.*

"Slay, girl, slay!" Callie says as we bump hips on the way to the costume shop.

It makes no sense for Callie and me to direct *and* act in the show we wrote, but it's fun. For Callie, it's a chance to add "director" to her résumé. And with a bossy mouth like hers, it's wild that she *hasn't* directed anything so far. For me, it's more about getting to play whichever part I want. In other words, I finally get to play a goddamn woman: Miranda.

In the original *Tempest,* Prospero conjures up a magic storm to shipwreck his enemies on the island where he lives in exile with his daughter, Miranda. He basically spends the whole play fucking with everybody until he gets to be the Duke of Milan again.

In our version, Miranda is a trans girl, living on an isolated homestead, who summons a storm of thunder, lightning, and rain whenever Prospero deadnames her. (Though Prospero thinks he's the one doing it, the arrogant prick.) Mr. Walker suggested adapting a play that already messes with gender, like *Twelfth Night* or *As You Like It*. But in those shows, the characters swap genders like costumes and everyone ends up cis and straight in the end. *No thanks, Tom Hanks.* On the other hand, *The Tempest* is about confinement, self-determination, and revenge—arguably the most trans attributes known to humankind.

Callie's playing Ariel, the magical, nonbinary spirit bound to serve Prospero. In our version, Ariel was rescued not from a bewitched tree but from a gender binary that doesn't allow them to express their true self. We tried to shoehorn Callie in as Caliban, if only because of the name connection. But we didn't want to deal with Caliban's whole I-want-to-rape-Miranda thing, so we just cut him from the plot.

We're not in dress rehearsals yet, but I grab the braided gold headband from my garment bag to keep the bangs out of my face. My hair is too short to pull back and too long to be anything but a hot mess. And maybe I like how the headband makes my eyes "extra hazel-y," as Martín puts it. He plays Miranda's love interest, Ferdinand. Martín is very hot but, unfortunately for me, very gay.

"Looks like everyone's here except Miles," Callie says, looking around. Miles plays Prospero, so we can't really start without him. "Can someone go find him?"

"No need," a voice booms from the hallway, and Miles appears. Miles is also hot but, unfortunately for me, a huge asshole. "Here I am. Ready, Ham-Glam?"

My stomach flips upside down. Ham-Glam is the nickname

my castmates gave me during *Hamlet* after I jokingly wore a gaudy sequined corset from the costume closet during rehearsal. I wasn't out to most people as trans back then, so it's a nickname for a gay guy.

"Miles, I'm tired of reminding you," Callie barks. Girl can *shout* when she wants to.

"Come on," Miles says, rolling his eyes. "Ham-Glam is gender neutral."

"It's Lucy, or Miranda during rehearsal." Callie to my rescue. No hesitation. No side glances at me to make sure she's being a good ally.

"Sorry, *Miranda*." Miles puts on a mock-serious face. "Daughter. Fruit of my loins . . ."

I roll my eyes, easy, breezy, unbothered.

"Yeah, also never say *loins* again," Callie adds.

Now that all six of us actors are here, we play a warm-up game called zip zap zoom. I can't focus and am the first person out. As I wait for the game to finish, I try to ready my brain for rehearsal, but it keeps wandering into college territory. What if Miles applies to Hughes next year? I picture myself walking through campus, hearing an unexpected "Hey, Ham-Glam!" as I turn a corner. When it comes to managing my gender dysphoria, one comment can quickly escalate into a ninety-five-car pileup. At Central, will I always be waiting for that next crash?

We run lines until Mr. Walker lets us know that the stage is free. Backstage, I shake my head, jump up and down, wiggle my appendages, and buzz my lips. I'm ready.

Our characters Alonsa, Ferdinand, and Stephanie sit in three chairs meant to suggest a car. On opening night, we'll have sound effects and lights to show that they're driving through a thunder-storm, but for now, Callie just shouts, "BOOM, FLASH, PITTER-PATTER!" from the front row.

"Eyes on the road, Stephanie!" wails Alonsa, a middle-aged tech tycoon. She's played by Shireen, a junior who went off book a week into rehearsals. *Legendary.*

"I'm trying, boss!" screeches Stephanie, her underpaid assistant. "I can't see a thing!" Emma's a sophomore with purple hair, who's going to whip out a knitting project the moment her character exits the scene.

"I'm gonna be sick," moans Ferdinand, Alonsa's son. He's played by Martín, the aforementioned hot gay guy—a senior.

"Why your cousin insisted on getting married in rural Pennsylvania I'll never know," Alonsa mutters to herself.

"It was a beautiful wedding, though, wasn't it?" Ferdinand muses.

Emerging from stage left, Prospero raises his staff and says in his booming voice, "Thunder! Wind! Lightning! Rain down on my enemies!" He lowers his voice and says over his shoulder, "Pretty impressive, don't you think, Randolph?"

I step out from the wings and roll my eyes with my entire body. "For the millionth time, Dad, my name is *Miranda*," I say. After the Ham-Glam comment, sounding annoyed doesn't take much acting.

"BOOM!" Callie shouts.

Prospero deflates and heaves a huge sigh. "Son, you've never even *met* a girl. You couldn't possibly know what it means to *be* one." Miles delivers the line while staring directly into my eyes.

I fall to my knees. "You're not listening to me!" I yell. We've rehearsed this scene dozens of times, but the frustration jolts through my body as if I'm living it for the first time.

"BOOM! CRASH!" Callie bellows. As Miranda's agony intensifies, so does the storm.

"Aaahhh!" the three travelers scream in unison. Stephanie gives the invisible steering wheel a sharp turn, and the three of them fall over together as if their car has crashed into a ditch. *Nice.* We spent half an hour last week perfecting that moment.

"Ferdinand? Where are you, honey?" Alonsa calls, squinting and stretching her arms out in front of her.

"Mom?" Ferdinand calls back. "I'm over here! I can't see anything!"

"Finally," Stephanie says with a deep sigh. "Time for happy hour." She pulls a mini bottle of "tequila" from her purse and tips it back. "If I have to spend one more minute with that woman, I'm going to lose my mind."

"Everything is going according to plan, Randolph," Prospero says, patting me on the back.

Miles's hand sends a jolt of rage through me. *Don't touch me!* I want to shout. Even though I'm the one who wrote that stage direction.

"BOOM!" Callie shouts.

My mind goes blank. *What is wrong with me?* "Line?"

Zak, our stage manager, prompts from the wings: "I know who I am . . ."

"Right, right, right. Got it." I continue the scene. "I know who

19

I am, Father, and my name is Miranda. And I don't understand why you're delighting in the torment of these travelers."

"Ahh, now *that* calls for a story," Prospero says, rubbing his hands together.

Shit, shit. My mind is a spinning wheel of death. *Program quit unexpectedly, rebooting.*

"Miranda?" Callie says after a few seconds of me looking stupid. "You're forgetting lines that *you* wrote. Are you okay?"

"Sorry," I say.

Mr. Walker sits in the middle of the auditorium, his fingers pressed together in front of his mouth. *I have to show him I can play a woman.* For our freshman show, *Pinocchio,* I requested the role of Blue Fairy on my audition form. In *Beauty and the Beast,* it was Mrs. Potts. In *Hamlet,* Ophelia. Every show I've tried out for, I've asked for a female role, but Mr. Walker always cast me as a man, or an enchanted cheese grater at best. It's not like I told him I *wasn't* a boy until last year. But writing a kick-ass trans woman into our play doesn't do much good if I forget my own lines.

Callie must notice my existential crisis, because she says, "Let's take a five-minute break."

I exhale in relief and ignore Mr. Walker's gaze. Callie and I head back to the costume shop, this time to our favorite gold velour couch. I call it the Therapy Couch. It's actually where I came out to Callie as trans, back when we were wee little freshies. The support beam under the cushions has been broken since circa 1998, so it literally sucks you inside. It's the closest you'll get to a private retreat around here.

"What's going on, Luce?" Callie asks, swapping her bossy

20

director voice for an I'm-here-for-you tone. "You've seemed out of it since Saturday."

I shrug, waiting for her to untangle my nonwords.

"Is this about the Central tour?" she asks. "Because Ben and Lewis are fuckups."

"I know they are," I say, not answering her question. Because I *am* still shaken up from the tour but mad that I'm letting it get to me.

"I heard they took career aptitude tests and got—well, guess what careers they got."

"Um, telemarketers?"

"No."

"Porta potty installers?"

"Almost."

"The guys who slurp poop out of porta potties after they're full?"

"Yeah, but with their *mouths.*"

I smile, and she rests her head on my shoulder. "And I'm really sorry for bringing up *Hamlet* the way I did. I ruined the whole tour for you," she says. "I'm like Jude Law betraying Jesus over here."

"Judas."

"Yes! That's what I meant. Which makes you . . ."

"Jesus, Callie, you didn't do anything—"

"Yep, Jesus. That's the one. You're Jesus, and I'm Judas."

I crack a smile. This is what I love. The two of us sinking into this sorry excuse for furniture and saying the stupidest shit we can think of.

"I hope I didn't wreck, like, the whole college thing for you."

"You didn't," I say. "It's not even about that. It just—" My throat closes up as I try to tell her that the Dream doesn't fit me the way it used to. "Central wasn't what I'd hoped it would be."

"I mean, it was a pretty shitty choice to not even *mention* the build-your-own-waffle bar on the tour, I get it." She's smirking. "Tell me more, though."

I shrug. "I thought college would be a fresh start. But I'm getting the feeling it's just going to be high school all over again." I lay my head back on the couch. "Being trans is so hard sometimes."

Callie pulls me into a tight side hug. "Good thing I'm around. I'll hunt down anyone who hurts you and smash them into hummus, okay?"

"Did you think it was weird that students don't get to direct a real show until senior year?" I ask.

Callie shrugs. "Not on the main stage. But maybe you'd get to do shows in the black box theater?"

"Maybe."

Mr. Walker appears from behind a rack of tailcoats and top hats. "Knock knock."

We try to stand up, but the couch pulls us deeper into its cushioned clutches. "Sorry—we're coming," Callie says. "We just needed a little heart-to-heart."

"Girls." He drags over an antique trunk and sits on it. "I need a moment with you."

My heart crackles like a firecracker. I'm used to letting teachers down, but not Mr. Walker.

"Lucy was just—"

Mr. Walker holds up a hand. "This isn't about your lines." He looks at me. "Though some extra practice wouldn't hurt." He hands us a flyer. It says: *THE STORM: A Queer Retelling of Shakespeare's "The Tempest,"* with a background of blue, pink, and white storm clouds—the colors of the trans pride flag. It's the marketing flyer Callie and I designed and submitted to the principal's office for approval.

"Did they okay it?" Callie asks.

Mr. Walker frowns and gives his head a slow shake.

Fudge-covered fuck balls.

"You've got to be kidding me," Callie says, rocketing herself out of the couch and shaking the flyer. "What's wrong with it?"

"They've decided the word *queer* is offensive," Mr. Walker explains. "They also want you to change the background colors."

Anger shoots through my limbs. *"What?"* I say.

"What, they're banning pink, blue, and white?" Callie slaps the paper. "Since when is the color wheel a force for evil?"

Mr. Walker speaks through half-gritted teeth. "Apparently, the school board's new policy is to avoid political messages of any kind. Which, they've decided, includes the colors of a flag."

"That's totally fucked!" Callie adds, then covers her mouth. "Sorry, *fudged.*"

Mr. Walker doesn't flinch—just gives us a defeated look. "I agree. And I'm so sorry."

"But *why?*" I ask, my voice creaking to life.

"This is coming from those Frosted Flakes at the school board meetings, isn't it?" Callie says.

Last spring, Callie and I watched a board of education meeting online after we heard someone got arrested for throwing a chair at the superintendent. Hundreds of people had come to yell about the "disgusting" books available in the school libraries and class assignments that were supposedly designed to "brainwash" their children. Parents were furious their kids might find out that LGBTQ+ people and people of color exist, apparently. *The horror.*

Mr. Walker nods. "I think they're trying to tamp down new controversies before they come up."

But *The Storm* is something *we* made. Mr. Walker didn't force us to write about gender issues, and it's not like students can read our script in the library.

Callie waves the flyer like an old-timey paper boy hawking the news. "And they think *this* is a controversy?"

"I know it's not right, girls. But they've asked you to revise the flyer and resubmit it for approval."

I summon cumulonimbus clouds, rain, and lightning, until the roar of thunder drowns out all the sounds in my head.

3

AT HOME, I ZOMBIE-WALK TO THE
kitchen and flip on the electric kettle. I wouldn't
mind a joint right now, but a cup of tea will have
to do.

"How was your day, Lucy?" Mom asks. *Lucy.*
Never any fuss with her.

"Stressful," I say.

"Want to talk about it?"

I shake my head weakly. "Just more of the same," I say
vaguely.

And then the full weight of my own words hits me, heavier
than if the fridge had tipped right on top of me. "Just more of the
same" might be my whole future. Forever.

She must see the exhaustion in my face, because her voice softens. "What, honey? Tell me."

I know Mom would take my side on everything stressing me
out—the nonsense with our flyer, the disappointing Central tour,

the low-level harassment from kids like Lewis, Ben, and Miles. But unfolding all that trauma in front of Mom could send her into one of her can't-get-out-of-bed slumps. So I settle on just one piece. "The principal banned the flyer we made for our play. Apparently it's not allowed to say *queer* or have the colors of the trans flag."

"Oh, honey. That's not fair at all." She wraps me in a hug. "How can I help?"

I sigh. "We emailed the office saying that forcing us to change the flyer is a violation of our civil rights."

"That sounds reasonable. I'm sure they'll come around." Still hugging me, Mom rubs my shoulder blades in the spots that always get sore. I lower my head and relax into her flat chest. Mom only wears her prosthetics on special occasions, because they're uncomfortable, which feels like solidarity with me and my far-too-slowly-growing boobs.

I doubt they'll "come around," but maybe we can at least fight to keep the pink, blue, and white cloud background. Callie and I spent hours teaching ourselves graphic design, trying to get the effect just right.

"I want to worry about regular teenager stuff for once," I say. "Like pimples or whatever."

"Lucky for you, that estrogen has really cleared up your acne." She kisses my forehead.

She's right. After two years on hormones—or my titty Skittles, as I like to call them—my face has started glowing like the porcelain-faced vampire I truly am inside.

The front door slams, and Dad clomps into the kitchen with

his work boots. He's doing electrical work for construction sites right now. *Aaaand cut.* This touching scene is over.

"I'm home," Dad says. "How's everybody?" He finds so many creative ways to greet me without saying my name. Calling me and Mom *everybody* is better than him using my deadname, obviously. But a casual *Lucy* here and there would be nice.

"Good," I say, and force a smile.

Mom side-eyes me, opening the tea cupboard. "Green? I'll make it and bring it up."

"Thanks, Mom."

Upstairs, I put on my favorite flowery maroon dress, which so far I haven't been brave enough to wear off the premises but always makes me feel better. Once I'm comfortable, I turn on some Billie Eilish and nestle into my pillows.

When Mom drops off a mug of tongue-burning green tea with loads of honey, she stays to watch a few videos of cute cats and goats on my phone. I got her hooked on them during her treatments, when she was too exhausted to follow the plots of the *NCIS* episodes that seemed to play in a continuous loop.

When she leaves the room, her sunshine smile radiates so much acceptance that I almost forget everything else. But then I open my laptop, and the Hughes program application page accosts me like a church kid trying to get me to come to their youth group. The feeling of wrongness that I felt on the tour floods over me again. Is Central too close to home? Too full of high school bros? Too big to get time onstage or in the director's chair?

I've ignored wrongness before, when *boy* just didn't feel right growing up. And the truth about my gender had to come out in the end. Do the same rules apply for choosing a college?

In a new tab, I search *Best LGBTQ+ colleges*. Maybe the problem is that I've never really looked at other schools. Callie and I came up with the Dream before we even really knew there *were* other colleges. I click on an article about the top twenty-five colleges for queer students. Each entry gives a little overview of the school and has a link to the website. My GPA is too low for one. The next is so freaking expensive, I'd have to sell three kidneys to survive my freshman year. Another doesn't offer degrees in theater.

The very last school on the list catches my eye: Botetourt College. The picture shows an imposing brick building with white columns and a legit mountain range in the background. The sun is setting behind it and everything. I click to the school's website, which is covered in more pictures of the same mountain range, plus more historical buildings. It's a small college with just over a thousand students. (Central has forty-five thousand, for comparison.) Google Maps shows me that it's nestled in the Appalachian Mountains, six hours from here. I've never thought of going to school somewhere so far away. Even though Mom's in remission, the thought of being a half day's drive away makes my stomach do a somersault.

At the same time, this school looks fucking cool.

I find the theater-major page. (Cue my sigh of relief—this school I'm already falling in love with isn't too tiny for a theater program.) It's definitely smaller than Central's, but they still have one four-hundred-seat auditorium and a black box theater. They offer concentrations in acting, directing, tech, and playwriting. My mind whizzes with possibilities. Callie would have less competition for lead roles. There'd be fewer students competing for space on the stage to direct their own shows. And best of all, we'd be three hundred miles away from anyone we know from high school.

I click through the photo gallery and recognize a few of the productions. *9 to 5. Chicago. Legally Blonde.* Some of the photos are from shows I've never seen before: a line of women in military uniforms, a lanky girl covered head to toe in green feathers, a grandmother rocking what might be a baby raccoon in her arms. The only word I can think of is *fun.* Everyone's having an absolute blast. Callie would fit right in, I'm sure of it. I pick up my phone to call her but then hesitate.

Something feels different about this school.

I click back to the About page and read through several paragraphs of "reaching potential" and "shaping new leaders." It's not until I get to the bottom that I read it: "We pride ourselves on our tradition as a women's institution. . . ."

A women's college? Like, a finishing school for rich white girls? Whose fathers go to horse races on weekends? Whose mothers wear petticoats and plan benefit auctions? Those are still a thing?

I click back to the photo gallery and realize why the images felt unusual. Almost all the actors are women. But these girls don't look like they're taking classes about embroidery and salad forks. I low-key thought women's colleges went out of existence hundreds of years ago, but what do I know?

Something about this school feels absolutely right. I'm a woman. What better way to live as a woman than to earn a degree at a women's college?

LEAVING REHEARSAL ON TUESDAY, I HOP AND spin every few steps. We haven't heard anything back from the principal's office about the flyer, and I figure no news is good news. Excitement bubbles inside me like I have a new crush. But it's a crush on a school. A school I met on the internet.

"You're weirdly happy for someone being actively oppressed by her educational institution," Callie says. She's walking a few steps behind me, scribbling notes on her script with a stubby pencil.

Once I tell her about Botetourt, she'll forget all about our stupid flyer. It's time to set our sights on a more distant horizon. One with a mountain range.

It's now or never. I've got to tell her. "So, I was thinking . . ."

"Yeah?" Callie's forehead is wrinkled in concentration.

I suck in a big breath but chicken out. "You want a noncarbonated sugar water?" I say instead, gesturing to a vending machine.

Callie scrunches her nose. "No thanks. It's Dr Pepper or bust for me." The school vending machines only carry fruit punch, apple juice, and naturally and artificially flavored cranberry drink, all of which have been sitting there since circa 2008. *Oh, joy.*

We pass it without stopping, my heart racing. It's been like this all day, trying to tell Callie about Botetourt. It's like I'm trying to confess I kidnapped Meatball and am holding him for ransom.

Outside, we sit on the stairs to wait for Callie's stepbrother, Nikhil, to walk over from the middle school football field. My jacket zipper sticks as I bundle up. Callie lies out like she's sunbathing on the beach.

"Ahh," she sighs to the sky. "Soak into me, Madame Sun."

"It's cloudy," I point out.

"Fine." She spreads out further. "Soak into me, trace amounts of UV rays. That better?"

My hair falls into my face when I look down at her. *Just tell her.*

The doors crack open, and Deja and Carina walk out, laughing. *Welp.* Carina tosses her backpack onto the ground and sets a Bluetooth speaker on the top step. "Janelle Monáe coming your way," she announces.

The opening beats of "Tightrope" spill down the steps and soothe the jitters in my muscles. I stand up and let my body move. All four of us learned this dance back in elementary school. Callie and I watched the video on repeat for hours and even had these sparkly jackets we'd wear, with bow ties we made from bandannas. Little nine-year-old me loved how Janelle was so free and femme, even though they wore a suit and bow tie. They showed me that I could be femme even though I only wore boys' clothes. And when Janelle came out as nonbinary, we lost our minds.

I dance. Like, really dance, the way I never do without a couple of wine coolers from the back of a theater kid's fridge.

I yank Callie up, and we spin and twist together. What we lack in precision we make up for in enthusiasm.

Deja jumps up and dances beside us, even though she seems to have forgotten most of the moves. Carina sits next to her speaker, swaying.

My legs wiggle on their own, my eyes close, I smile. So what if the Dream has changed? Dreams are meant to change. In kindergarten, I thought I'd grow up to be the Little Mermaid. (Which, to be fair, would still be awesome if the opportunity presented itself.) Callie is going to understand. She's my best friend.

When "Tightrope" ends, I collapse on the cold steps, out of breath. "I haven't done that in a while," I say. And then, before I can chicken out, I lower my voice and blurt, "Callie, I need to talk to you. About Central."

Callie sits down next to me, and the opening beats of "Poker Face" spill from Carina's speaker. "Is this about the showcase?" Callie asks.

I swallow. "Not really. Just—do you think we need a backup school? What if we don't get in?"

"Did you do *that* bad on your physiology test?" Callie jokes.

"Just do your prereqs freshman year," Deja says from behind us. "That's what I'm doing. Then you can try out for Hughes again as a sophomore." Yep, Deja and Carina are going to Central, too. At this point they might as well convert our high school gym into a satellite campus.

"I say dream big," Callie says. "Is Hughes to be or not to be?" she projects in a Shakespearean voice. "Either way, we shall be together." She squeezes me around the shoulders.

Shit on a sandwich.

"Hey, are you guys going to that prospective-student weekend thing?" Deja asks.

Callie's eyes light up. "Yeah! Mr. Walker's letting us cancel practice that Friday night."

Central's prospective-student weekend is a chance for high school seniors to sleep over in the dorms and experience campus life. In theory, it would be a ton of fun. If I wasn't still washing the bad taste out of my mouth from our last visit.

"Sweet!" Carina says. "It's gonna be lit."

"Is *Othello* canceling that day, too?" I ask. Deja's playing Emilia, and Carina's playing Bianca.

"It's a leads-only practice," Deja says, making no attempt to hide the disappointment in her voice. She tried out for Desdemona, but Carlos cast his girlfriend in the role. Maybe we should've cast her as Prospero to avoid the headache known as Miles.

"Well, it sucks to suck, because the leads won't be eating a tower of waffles that weekend," Callie says.

WE HAVE A QUICK DINNER BREAK AT HOME,

and then it's time for work. I can't remember how Callie and I both ended up working at the orthodontist's. The person who hired us is, like, the wife of a friend of Callie's dad or something. Even though Callie lives three blocks away, she's fifteen minutes late. I've already sanitized all the dental chairs and started on the restroom when she bursts through the side door.

"Sorry I'm late, Luce. Meatball had a seizure, and there was *a lot* of puke."

"Again? Is he okay?"

"Yeah. He had convulsions on the kitchen floor for like thirty seconds, then just hopped up and went to his water bowl like nothing happened."

"What a trouper. I clocked you in."

"You're a lifesaver!" She hugs me.

We finish cleaning the dental chairs, emptying the trash, and vacuuming the carpet until the sharp tang of disinfectant has over-powered the sticky scent of children's spit. Time for phase two: working through the backlog of retainers, expanders, and mouth guards in the back room. Yep, they hired two teenagers as lab assis-tants. We only work at night and don't ask questions.

The deserted office is the perfect place to chat with Callie about Central. So, obviously, I blurt out something totally unre-lated. "The name-change fund just reached the halfway mark," I say, calculating last week's wages in my head.

I save what I can, but living as a girl is so *expensive.* There's always just one more piece you need for an outfit. A shirt is see-through and needs a camisole. Your slip-on shoes need special no-show socks. And makeup. *Oh my goddess.* And all the accessories to put the makeup on and take it off again.

"Ooh, yeah? And who are you today?"

"Lucy Josephine," I say, turning over the middle-name idea in my mouth like a fancy chocolate truffle. Mom says Josephine would've been my name if I'd been born a cis girl. I think it's classy, but I'm not sure I want the constant reminder of who I could have been.

Callie raises an eyebrow from behind her oversized safety glasses. "Hmm. I liked Lucy Cassiopeia better."

"You can change *your* middle name to Cassiopeia," I say. "I like the alliteration: Callie Cassiopeia."

"Look at you, Miss ACT vocab list. Is your backup school Harvard?"

I cringe, but Callie's already powering up the wet sand wheel and exhaust fan. She's taking the messier job because she was late. The *whoosh*ing and *whirr*ing do nothing to drown out the anxiety tornado spinning in my head.

"Can you choose a delicious specimen for us, Lucy *Josephine*?" Callie asks dramatically.

I take stock of the day's unpolished goods—dozens of pink plaster mouths fitted with colorful acrylic-and-wire devices. I choose a bright pink glitter retainer, exactly the kind I would've loved as a kid if I hadn't been keeping my girlness secret. I lift the upper retainer off the mold and hand it to Callie, who's wetting the pumice with a squirt bottle.

"Almost forgot—we need some tunes!" she announces. "Do you mind?" She holds up her fingers, which are already covered in a squishy gray mess of wet pumice.

I switch on the lab room speakers, connect my phone to the Bluetooth (it's called Blue 🦷 Speaker, obviously), and play some more Janelle Monáe. This afternoon's dance session got me in the mood. The volume is blasting to compete with the noise from the pumice wheel and fan.

"That's cool that Deja and Carina are going to Central, too," Callie shouts over the noise. "Maybe we could all get a suite together."

"Yeah." And it *is* cool, I guess. They've never been anything but supportive of me, before and after I came out. They'd be my allies at college, no question. And I know for a fact that Carina has a huge widescreen TV she'd bring along.

When Callie finishes the first stage of polishing, I power up the cloth wheel and prime it with a polishing stick. She wipes off the pink retainer and hands it to me, and I rub it against the wheel in small circles, taking off the cloudiness and coaxing out a deep, brilliant shine. If these things weren't destined for kids' mouths, they'd make great Christmas ornaments.

After work, Callie and I hang out in the park across the street, passing a joint back and forth. Callie has so many friends, she can always find someone's older sibling to buy weed from.

"Is this backup school about the flyer thing?" Callie asks as I take a drag. "Because if we let the school freak us out, we're letting them win. There's no way they can force us to change the name of our own show. We could totally sue."

I blow the smoke out slowly, trying to gather the courage to tell her what's on my mind. "It's not the show." *Say it say it say it say it say it.* "It's just—something felt off on the Central tour." My stupid eyes well up with stupid tears. "I, um, didn't like the school after all. At least what we saw."

Callie's face falls. My throat constricts, and I start coughing. Of course, I don't have my water bottle with me. She smacks me on the back and asks, "What in the hard-shell beef taco are you talking about?"

After I collect myself, I say, "What if we got a fresh start, Cal? Somewhere new?"

She gapes. "Central *is* a fresh start. A fresh start where we get to be roommates and eat Cheez Whiz nachos at midnight and make out with hot techies in the theater sound booth." The joint smolders between her fingers for a few moments.

"I know. But couldn't we do that somewhere else?" *Fucking say it.* "I've been looking at a college down south."

Her forehead wrinkles. "Down *south*? What, like Maryland?"

36

"No, like, *south*er. Virginia. It's called Botetourt College." I pronounce it slowly, the way I practiced: Bot-uh-*tot*, not bot-uh-*tort*.

"How far is that?"

"Like, five or six hours." I shrug, like I could drive that distance any day of the week.

She lets out a low whistle. "Do your parents know? Because they are literally going to have heart attacks and die."

"I haven't told them." But Callie's right. They've been a bit . . . overprotective since I came out. Which I get. Dad made the mistake of visiting the "list of people killed for being transgender" article on Wikipedia, and my freedoms went downhill from there. Mom's frequent hospital visits at the time didn't help.

"Like, you'd have to major in necromancy so you could bring them back to life," Callie adds.

"I'll check on Botetourt's witchcraft department when I get home." My face heats up from awkwardness, and I drag a stick through the dirt for something else to focus on. "Um, one supercool thing is that it's a women's college, which means—"

"Sorry, it's a *what*?"

"A . . . women's college?"

She cups a hand over her ear as if she can't hear me properly. "I'm sorry, did you say *cult*?"

"It's a real school," I say.

"Really. What do people major in? Salad forks?"

"They have an amazing theater program."

"Yeah, I bet the students are great actors. They're out there acting like they're *not* in a cult." She shakes her head, laughing to herself.

I laugh, too, even though it contradicts my point. "Lots of people go to women's colleges. Like Wellesley and Smith and all those." I shrug again, like I didn't just learn the names of those schools this afternoon.

"Who's Wellesley and Smith?" Callie demands.

I roll my eyes. "Famous women's colleges. Hillary Clinton went to Wellesley."

Callie rolls her eyes right back at me. "Sure, in like 1897."

"Well, lots of women still go to them." I pull up the Botetourt website on my phone and show it to her. She scrolls, scowling. "Nobody would question my gender if I studied there," I explain.

"Oh." Callie raises an eyebrow, intrigued all of a sudden.

"And the campus is really beautiful. There are *mountains*. And way less snow in the winter. We could go hiking and stuff." What am I saying? We hate hiking. But I can't stop rambling.

Callie frowns at me. "We?"

The word drops like a piece of plywood scenery falling over. *She doesn't want to go. Of course she doesn't.* "Well. Our pact has always been to go together. So hypothetically?" I stammer. "The theater program is so, so cool. I don't know—I feel like you might like it."

She's silent for a few moments, and I start rambling again. "It's a lot smaller than Central. We'd actually have a chance to be in shows, even as freshmen. Maybe even write and direct! Which we know wouldn't happen at Hughes until we're seniors." *Why is my breath catching in my throat like I'm fucking up a Broadway audition?*

Callie doesn't have a hint of playfulness on her face or sarcasm in her voice. It's unusual enough to spook me. "We just never talked about it, that's all. And aren't private schools, like, a million dollars a year?"

Obviously, I looked into that. "They give way more scholarships than Central does. Plus we'll get money from the government for being poor. It might end up costing about the same as Central." Mom filled out my FAFSA form as soon as it went live on October first. At least something good will come out of her not being able to work full-time anymore.

Callie laughs. "Thank god for being poor." Then she takes a deep breath. "But seriously. Can you picture yourself there?"

I close my eyes and imagine walking onto campus for the first time. Introducing myself as Lucy, and nobody giving my name a second thought. No one squinting at me, trying to remember which elementary school classroom they know me from. Starting from scratch with new friends and new teachers. "When I think about it, I imagine a blank canvas."

"An empty stage," Callie adds.

I open my eyes, smiling. "Exactly."

BACK AT HOME, I COLLAPSE INTO BED AND stalk the internet for more information about Botetourt. The town it's in is small, but it has some stuff Callie might like—a few cute coffee shops, an art museum, and even a queer nightclub. And lots of hiking. Maybe we could get into that after all.

A text pings in from Callie.

Callie: I'm looking at the site now

Callie: You're right

Callie: It does look pretty cool

I let out a breath I didn't know I was holding.

Me: Right??

Callie: Even though the all-girls thing is still weird

Me: Yeah it is

Me: But maybe it's good weird

Callie: But question tho

Callie: Don't get mad

Me: I won't

Callie: Are you 100% sure they'll let you in?

Callie: Like, do they have a trans policy?

The message punches me in the gut. But the school wouldn't be on a list of LGBTQ+ friendly colleges if they weren't T-friendly, too. Right?

Callie: Obv they SHOULD let you in and we'll sue the pants off em if they don't

Callie: I'll represent you in court

Callie: But still

I shoot off a question to the internet: *Can trans women go to women's colleges?*

I feel like a troll even typing it. Of course they can. *Right?* I click the first result: a Wikipedia article about transgender admissions policies at women's colleges. In 2013, a trans woman was denied admission to Smith because her identity was listed as male on the FAFSA. *Shit, am I listed as male on the FAFSA?* But then Smith revised their policy to officially allow trans women. Okay then, it's fine. Right?

But it worries me that 2013 isn't all that long ago, in the grand scheme of things. And Smith is just one school. There's no federal law saying a women's college has to let me in.

The article mentions a few other universities, but I do a Ctrl+F search for Botetourt and don't find anything.

Callie: Luce

Callie: Lucy Josephine

Callie: MADAME LUCY JOSEPHINE MYERS THE ENCHANTING

Me: WHAT!

Callie: Are you mad at me for asking that?

I ignore her for now and adjust my search: *Can trans women go to Botetourt?*

Headlines flood the screen: *Botetourt students protest trans student policy* and *Transgender men couldn't graduate from a women's college in . . .*

My throat constricts, and I exit the page. My brain cannot process those headlines right now.

Me: Sorry, was researching

Me: Then I saw transphobic stuff and panicked

I pull up my favorite baby sloth compilation video to detox. One of the poor babies has casts on its little baby sloth arms, which makes my problems feel smaller.

Callie: No prob

Callie: Detective Cal is on the case

While Detective Cal saves me from tumbling down a transphobia rabbit hole, I go to Instagram and look for pretty pictures of Botetourt's campus. I scroll through shots of the quaint brick buildings backdropped with stunning mountainscapes and pastel skies. College-aged women clinking champagne glasses on the grassy quad. A three-person kick line doing some sort of pajama dance in a dorm hallway. And then two actresses in stage makeup, looking dramatically at an open, empty suitcase, stage mics delicately tucked against their cheeks. From the description, it looks like the shot is from a dress rehearsal for last year's spring show. I tap the username @thesp_ian and scroll through the photos. Surprisingly, this person seems to be a guy. Maybe he works there? He looks way too young to be a professor, though.

I scroll through several more shots of the same show. One is a backstage selfie of @thesp_ian in a black V-neck.

A perfectly tight black V-neck.

I blink the fluttering thought away. Black tees make every techie look a little sexy, regardless of their inherent hotness, and I don't have the emotional bandwidth to support an internet crush right now.

Still, I check out his profile. His name is Ian Bianco-Chan, and his bio says he's a theater nerd and avid hiker. Lots of his pictures are theater photos, many with his arms around his mom. I check Botetourt's faculty list, and sure enough, there's her smiling face. Marcy Chan, professor of theater.

Interesting.

I think about texting Callie about him but stop. She'll take one look at his V-neck—she knows my weakness—and assume I'm developing feelings that might cloud my college decision. But I just want to know more about the theater program.

So I type him a message.

Hey! So, you don't know me, but I'm thinking about applying to Botetourt. . . .

Then I erase it, because since when am I a creepy stalker? Luckily, Callie sends me a text that startles me out of my love-crazed mission.

Callie: I've got good news and bad news and great news

Me: ???

Callie: Good news: trans students are allowed

Callie: I read the admissions policy

I groan with relief. *Thank fucking goddess.*

Callie: Bad news: I can't find anything about a trans woman ever going there

Me: Womp

Callie: At least you'd get to be #1?!

She sends a GIF of her hero, SpongeBob SquarePants, wearing a novelty drinking cap that says *#1* in big, red typeface.

> **Me:** Oh joy

> **Me:** But what's the great news?

Callie: Brace yourself

> **Me:** *Drumroll*

Callie: I have confirmed the existence of a waffle bar

I laugh out loud, I'm so relieved.

> **Me:** Woo!!

> **Me:** It's meant to be!!!!

My message sounds like a joke, but it's not. Discovering Botetourt feels like destiny. By now, I know I'm going to apply, like I know I'm going to lace up my fuchsia Converses tomorrow morning and eat two raspberry Pop-Tarts for breakfast. I just want Callie to feel the same way.

As soon as we're done chatting, I return to @thesp_ian's page. Who better to help me decide if Botetourt is a good fit? His mom works in the theater department, so he knows all the gossip and drama.

But first things first. Until I figure out how feasible it is for me to apply and get accepted as a trans girl, it's probably best if I go stealth. I open my own profile and scroll through the pictures. The first one is from the Central tour, when I was looking fly. *Okay, good start, girl.* Unsurprisingly, I have an absurd number of dim photos of Callie and me making goofy faces backstage. Many of them feature me after taking advantage of the stage makeup. *Cute!* I get lost remembering the fun times Callie and I have had in the theater.

But then one image slaps me in the face: I'm laughing hysterically in the Walmart checkout line, chin up and Adam's apple stabbing about three feet from my neck. *Gross.* A man had just let out a long, rumbly fart in the next line over, and Callie and I could not keep it together. It's a funny memory, but I don't exactly pass. Delete. A wave of guilt shudders over me, but I shrug it off.

I keep scrolling, deleting a bunch of pics from my early adventures in gender, before I can talk myself out of it. I save them to my phone, though. Even if they bring me dysphoria and would out me to @thesp_ian, those days were important. My eyes well up at the picture of Dad holding an *I Love My Transgender Daughter* sign at our first Pride March last summer. That day took a lot of work to get to, for both of us, and it hurts to pull it off my page. *Sigh.* But this is my fresh start. Maybe I'll put them back up someday.

I scrutinize my profile one more time. I find a stray comment from Callie—three cheese emojis and a trans pride flag—and delete it.

A thought flits into my head, and I quickly squash it: *You're censoring your profile, just like the school board wants you to censor the flyer.* Fuck you, brain. Shut the hell up.

It's complicated. I'm open about who I am, and the school board can't stop me from channeling pride into our showcase. I'm not ashamed of any of these photos, even if they out me. But it *is* nice to have the option to come out on my own terms—to live stealth as a cis girl until I choose to share my full identity. I'm keeping the photos that show a confident, mysterious woman. And that woman will still be trans and proud, even if she doesn't tell you right away.

I return to @thesp_ian's page and get lost in his kind eyes. Something about him feels familiar and right. Not quite the same way the name Lucy clicked into place, or the way I already felt at home when I first landed on Botetourt's homepage. But something in my gut tells me he could be a great friend.

I take one long, deep breath. I let it out slowly.

And before I can talk myself out of it, I message him.

ALL MORNING, MY BELLY SPINS

like clothes in a dryer. My message to @thesp_ian
is still marked as unread. But it's out of my hands
now.

My phone buzzes halfway through third period,
and I jump so high my knee jams into the desk. I pull
out my phone, but it's just an email. From the school. My
heart rate spikes.

From: Admin@Clayton.K-12.PA.org
To: LMyers@Clayton.K-12.PA.org; CKatz@Clayton.K-12.PA.org
CC: MWalker@Clayton.K-12.PA.org

Dear Callie and Lucy,

Thanks for expressing your disappointment regarding our
decision on your marketing flyer. We apologize for the incon-
venience, and we wish things were different. Here at Clayton

High School, we support the rights of our LGBTQ+ students and strive to be a place where all students feel a sense of belonging. Unfortunately, we are reaffirming our decision to reject the flyer, based on guidance from the Clayton City Schools Board of Education. We understand the frustration this may cause, but please know that our office will gladly assist you in revising the flyer to meet the requirements.

We have also been informed that a representative of the Clayton Board of Education plans to attend a rehearsal to review your show's content. Mr. Walker has supplied them with a rehearsal schedule and script. Please know that our office supports you, and we believe that trans lives matter.

Best,
Principal Calvin Schmidt
(he/him)

"Be yourself. Everyone else is already taken."

Dread floods through my chest, gut, arms, and legs. I start typing a Mayday message to Callie, but she beats me to it.

Callie: WE ARE GOING TO DIE!!! ☠

My thoughts exactly. At least if I'm dead, it won't matter if @thesp_ian thinks I'm an internet weirdo and never messages me back.

Me: We thought a fucking flyer was the worst of our problems

> **Callie:** We poked the beast

> **Callie:** Now they want BLOOD

There's no way they can force us to revise our show. What do they want us to do—write a whole new script and start over?

> **Me:** What are the chances they ask us to unqueer the show?

> **Callie:** I give it a transphobia percent chance with a side of fuck-them dipping sauce

IT TURNS OUT WE DON'T HAVE TO AGONIZE over the school board visit for long. Twenty minutes into this afternoon's rehearsal, a middle-aged white woman slips into the auditorium and takes a seat near the back. *Of course.* We're rehearsing one of the raunchiest scenes in the show today, when Ariel and Stephanie get drunk on mini tequilas that Stephanie stole from the rural Pennsylvania wedding. Instead of scrutinizing Callie's and Emma's blocking like I'm supposed to, I study this woman like she's a puzzle to solve. She's wearing an emerald button-down shirt with a bold flower pattern. It's *cute.* Someone that stylish can't be a complete bigot, can they?

"You're telling me," Ariel says drunkenly, legs dangling off the edge of the stage, "that your boss made you drive her and her son three hours into the middle of nowhere? For her *niece's wedding*?"

Ariel shakes their head, chuckling. "Girl, you do *not* get paid enough for that."

There's no way Callie's seen School Board Karen, because she's slurring her words with *way* too much enthusiasm.

Stephanie nods. "Yup. For minimum wage." At first glance, Emma isn't the actor I'd expect to play the role of an alcoholic wannabe comedian. She's the youngest and shyest of the cast and admitted at our first read-through that she'd rather watch anime in her pajamas than set foot near a high school kegger. But this girl comes alive onstage. Her slurring is so realistic that I start to suspect there's really tequila in those bottles.

I glance back at Karen, but I can't read her expression.

"What about you?" Stephanie asks, leaning back on her hands. "You're a magical spirit, but you're basically an unpaid intern."

"Yeahhhh. But the thing is, Prospero rescued me from imprisonment." Ariel heaves a sigh. "So there's this whole I-owe-my-life-to-him thing."

"Imprisoned by . . . ?" Stephanie trails off.

Ariel collapses onto their back, raises their arms wide, and wails, "The gender binary!"

My head whips to Karen, whose face I can sure as hell read now. She raises her eyebrows and purses her lips in shock, as if Callie just farted in her face.

"My entire life I've been uncomfortable in my body." Ariel stands up and does a spirited interpretive dance around the stage. "So Prospero transformed me into an agender, ethereal being, and I've never felt more like myself."

Karen's brain is probably falling out of her butt right now.

51

"What are your pronouns?" Stephanie asks.

"They/them," Ariel says.

I cringe. Parents love to scream about pronouns at school board meetings, as if a part of speech could invade their neighborhood and burn down their homes at any moment.

"Sweet. She/her for me," Stephanie responds. She pulls two more mini bottles from her bag and hands one to Ariel. They twist them open, clink them together, and throw back the drinks with the effortlessness of fraternity bros.

Karen scribbles on her notepad like she has thirty seconds left to finish a physics final.

We. Are. Fucked.

AFTER PRACTICE, CALLIE AND I COLLAPSE INTO the Therapy Couch. I lean on her shoulder and let out an agonized groan. "We're *doomed*."

Callie runs her fingers through my hair. "That buttered-bread-faced bitch can write whatever she wants on a clipboard, but she is *not* raining out our show. That's Miranda's job."

I force a half laugh, but it sounds like it comes from a crusty mummy.

Callie elbows me. "Hey. I have something to cheer you up." She opens her notebook, showing what looks to be a shopping list.

Cute dress

Statement necklace

Interview shoes

Businessy jacket

Gummy worms

Tiny muffins with tiny chocolate chips in tiny single-serve packs

Killer playlist

She looks at me expectantly.

"I didn't know you still wrote letters to Santa," I say.

She drops the notebook with mock exasperation. "It's a shopping list. For our *road trip*."

"What road trip?"

"To Bort-a-Toot, you dum-dum," she says, mispronouncing Botetourt on purpose. "When I was researching last night, I saw that there's a prospective-student weekend coming up. Just like the one at Central. They'll feed us and everything!"

Us. My heart gallops. "You'd go with me? Seriously?"

"Seriously," she says. "With all this bullshit going on, it really made me question where I want to spend the next four years of my life. Maybe it'd be better to go to a small school after all." Her shoulders sink. "And I'm sorry for saying Booty-Butt is a cult and all that. I should've heard you out."

I try to slow down my racing heart. "Just because I'm thinking of applying doesn't mean you have to, too." *But how amazing would it be if she did?*

"That's the point of visiting, right?" Callie says. "So I can decide whether I want to? I'm not saying I'm ready to give up the Dream. But maybe we can, you know, revise it."

Oh my goddess, oh my goddess. "Cal, a road trip would be unbelievably fun and amazing and cool." Like a little slice of college while we're still trapped in the toxic waste pit known as high school. "I'm going to pee my pants, I'm so excited." I wrap her in a hug and squeeze. She squeals and hugs me back.

"So when is it?" I ask, out of breath with excitement.

"Oh shoot, I forget."

I navigate to the website on my phone and check their admissions calendar. A banner across the top of the page says *Prospective Students Weekend,* with the dates underneath. I don't know how I missed it before. But then a spike drills into my heart. "It's the same weekend as Central's, Cal. It starts on Friday and everything."

"Are you kidding me?" She grabs the phone and stares at the screen. "Fu-u-u-uck."

I sink into the couch, letting it consume me. "Welp. Scratch that."

"Wait," Callie says.

"Cal, there's no way. Don't even talk about it."

"Hypothetically, though, what if—"

"We are *not* skipping Central's," I interrupt. "You started wiggling your arms like SpongeBob SquarePants when you first heard about it. I'm not taking that away from you."

Callie holds her arms out in a T and then wiggles them like she's underwater. "Well, guess what? I'm wiggling my arms for Boot-Scootin'-Boogie College, too. How 'bout that?"

I sigh. "It's a six-hour drive. Our folks are never gonna go for it." But even as my mouth moves, my mind races to think of a way to make this work.

THAT NIGHT, I LIE ON MY BED WITH ALL THE lights on. The fan on my warm laptop whirs as I click through Botetourt's web page for the seven millionth time. With my other hand, I lift my phone every five seconds to make sure I haven't missed an email from the school board or principal.

There's no way they're going to let us advertise the show now. Maybe they'll even restrict our performance to just the theater classes or something. It's not like the senior showcases ever sell out the auditorium. But still, it would've been cool to share our work with the world.

We should've just revised the flyer.

Ding. The vibration sends a jolt through my hand, and the phone flies out of my grip. But when I pick it up, there's no email notification.

It's a message from @thesp_ian.

> **@thesp_ian:** Hey Lucy! Sure, I'd love to tell you about Botetourt. My mom's a professor here. Do you have any specific questions?

When the next notification dings in, I collapse onto the floor as if it's a fainting couch.

@thesp_ian started following you.

55

5

"MAYBE WE COULD MAKE A TRIP

to Botetourt work after all," I say to Callie the
next day. We haven't heard a peep from the school
board or Principal Schmidt. But @thesp_ian and I
have already exchanged more words over text than my
parents and I speak to one another in a week. He has
tons to say about Botetourt—the culture, the theater, the
surprise holiday every fall when classes are canceled and the
entire student body hikes a mountain in ridiculous costumes.
I'm pretty sure I have a guaranteed friend in town, which makes
going to school out of state seem safer.

Callie squeals. "Eeeeehhhh! Road trip!" She deflates a bit. "But
I had a whole speech planned to help convince you."

I roll my eyes. "All right, pretend I said that I refuse to go."

Callie clears her throat and takes a deep, dramatic breath.
"Think about Miranda. She's imprisoned on her cozy homestead
with a controlling dad who doesn't respect her pronouns and bosses

his nonbinary spirit minion around with no regard for their work-life balance." Callie uses her deepest voice, narrator-style. "And Miranda could stay there forever, rent-free with a meal plan. But she doesn't. You know why? Because she knows she's destined for something bigger."

I laugh. "That's the cheesiest shit I ever heard."

"We love cheese."

"Okay, you win," I say with mock reluctance. I'm about to open my mouth to spill the beans about Ian, but something makes me stop. The secret is too new and fragile. Plus Callie might get the idea that *he's* the reason I want to visit Botetourt in the first place. Which he's not. He's more like a hidden friendship bracelet at the bottom of a cereal box.

As I wait for English to start, I shoot Ian a message.

> **@lucygoosey:** I HAVE NEWS ●●

> **@lucygoosey:** I may or may not be coming down for a visit

It only takes a minute for him to respond. My belly flutters with the wings of a thousand tiny moths as I open his message.

> **@thesp_ian:** Are you serious?? That's amazing!

> **@thesp_ian:** Can I show you around?

> **@lucygoosey:** Umm, yes please

> **@thesp_ian:** Perf. Consider me your personal tour guide. Mostly high schoolers come to those prospie weekends, but I can give you the advanced tour

Huh? I'm not sure what he's talking about, as much as I love the offer. I send a vague joke back, hoping it makes sense.

> **@lucygoosey:** Yes, I think I will test out of the introductory tour 😕

> **@thesp_ian:** lol

> **@thesp_ian:** We don't get a ton of theater transfers

I scroll back through our messages, trying to figure out what he's talking about. *Why does he think I'm a transfer student?*

I find the culprit a few dozen messages back. I wrote: I just don't feel right about Central anymore. I'm looking for something new.

Then I glance through my remaining Instagram photos. There's nothing explicitly high-schooly about them, I guess.

Shi-i-i-it. He thinks I *already go* to Central. Like I'm a sophomore or something. *Why else would he be talking to a high schooler, ya dum-dum.* He's funny. He's talented. There's no way he'd befriend me if he knew I was still sleeping in my childhood twin bed every night, surrounded by my pile of beady-eyed plushies.

> **@lucygoosey:** I've got a good feeling about Botetourt. Don't wanna waste college fucking around at Central.

58

My heart races as I press send. It's not a lie if he's the one who said it. Right?

THAT SATURDAY, I PICK UP CALLIE, AND WE

drive to the thrift store across town. Callie would rather lick sand than buy herself new clothes, but she loves shopping for me.

"A fresh start calls for fresh outfits," she announces, as if I need convincing. "Or at least fresh-to-you outfits." She hoists her bare feet onto the dashboard and picks pink sock fuzz from between her toes. Callie might not survive with a college roommate other than me. She'd be an immediate target for murder.

Our local thrift shop is mostly bullshit, but being desperate for cute, cheap clothes has made me an expert fashion hunter. We push through the racks of musty blazers and pilly sweaters and stumble into the section I think of as Vintage Narnia. A mannequin in a flapper dress and hat stands in the center, encircled at the base by shiny stilettos and boots sparkling like a marquee. Band T-shirts from the eighties line one wall, and another is draped in floral parkas and fur trench coats. A jewelry counter glimmers under the fluorescent lighting with a collection of deliciously ostentatious brooches and oversized necklaces.

Callie dives right into the shoes. "What size again?"

I tell her. "But I can squeeze down to something smaller if they're cute enough." It's always tough finding stuff in my size, especially shoes.

I breathe in the delectable smell of old people and feet, fiddle with the flapper mannequin's bead necklace, and peruse the accessories. None of the simple chain-and-pendant necklaces jump out at me. But then my fingers find a vintage cameo, gold around the edge with a white carved profile of a young woman inside. Something about it calls to me.

"Don't you think she looks like Miranda?" I ask Callie.

"You know she's a fictional character, right? In a play with no illustrations?" Callie grabs the pendant and squints at it. "But she kind of looks like *you*. Which is about as Miranda-y as she could get."

I smile and keep the necklace. Now I need an outfit to go with it.

Each dress on the rack has its own history. What vibe fits me? I've only really had a year of full-time ladyhood to figure that out. Being raised as a boy, it's like I missed out on some ancestral knowledge of what patterns clash, what colors go with my skin tone, which cuts hide or accentuate which features. I get that other women have bad outfit days. But for me, a fashion mishap quickly spirals into a dysphoria disaster where I'm convinced that everyone is staring, judging, and calling me a pretender. (Apparently I had an "old lady" aesthetic early on, because floral shirts happen to be very cozy and often on sale.) Thank goddess for YouTube tutorials.

Now I try to just stick to a few styles that I know look good on me, even if I can't explain why they work. I linger on an A-line leather dress that might turn me into a warrior princess (but is too bold for me), pass on an ombré pink sweater dress someone's grandma made in knitting club, consider a gorgeous yellow sundress but then think of the weather, and finally find it: a green flowing dress that will perfect my forest-nymph persona. The cameo sets it off perfectly.

Then I go back to the leather dress and grab it, because I'm a grown-ass lady and can wear what I want.

"Are you looking for anything?" I ask Callie gently, thinking of the stinky cardigan she wore to the Central visit.

"Ugh. Asha just made me go buy black interview pants last weekend. I need a thirty-day reprieve before I set foot in another dressing room."

I grab a few more things and then head out of Narnia to the dressing rooms. I'll need to alter the green one, but it's nothing I can't handle. Mom taught me how to sew as a kid, when I wanted to make dresses for my stuffed animals. (How my parents were shocked when I came out continues to baffle me.) The warrior princess dress fits great, and the way I look in the mirror kind of scares me. In a sexy way.

I tuck the leather dress under the green one and step out, and Callie holds up a gray sweatshirt. Printed on the front is a dachshund in a hot dog bun, its tongue lolling out.

"What do you think? Greatest sweatshirt ever or just second best? It must be top two." Callie pulls it over her head, elated. She buys it, of course.

I use my entire paycheck on the haul, which means there's nothing to add to the name-change fund for now. But if I can wear these outfits to our Botetourt visit, the money is an investment in my future.

Back in Callie's bedroom, she flops onto the bed and watches me model all my possible outfit combinations. She says "slay" to everything I show her, which boosts my confidence but doesn't actually help with a decision. No, we have not asked our parents if we can set out on a cross-country road trip. But this adventure has already become the Plan with a capital *P*.

"Okay, pros and cons of us going to Bort-a-Toot," Callie says, holding up a notebook and pen.

"Bot-uh-tot," I correct her. I know she's joking, but I have yet to hear her pronounce it right, so she might actually be confused.

Callie scribbles in the notebook. "Pro. You get a fresh start. New state, new school, new you." She draws a line down the middle of the page. "And then the most obvious con. We'll be a five-hour-and-fifty-five-minute drive from Meatball."

On cue, Meatball jumps into her lap and gives her a sloppy kiss on the face.

"Yes, we're talking about you," Callie coos, scratching him behind the ears. "*Yes,* you hold the Guinness World Record for best doggo in the world. Stop asking me that."

Meatball's tail wags in approval.

"And another pro," I say. "My gender will go unquestioned."

Callie scribbles that on the pro side. "That does sound like a nice change of pace."

"And a con," I add. "The wrong person could figure out I'm trans, rumors could spread, parents might riot with torches, the school might burn down, I could be thrown into the flames and burned to a crispy strip of bacon."

Callie rolls her eyes but scribbles what I said on the con side. To Meatball, she murmurs, "That sounds like a great idea for our next play, huh? You wanna be an angry townsperson, baby?" She switches back to her normal voice to say, "But do you really think people would find out? Like, I know it's problematic to talk about trans people passing or not passing." Callie gets an A+ in remembering my lectures. "But I think you usually *do* pass, you know? Like, that estrogen has really been going to town on your face."

Even though I agree—I should feel valid as a woman whether I pass as cis or not—it still gives me a little boost of confidence to hear Callie's perspective. My makeup practice is paying off. "But I won't want to keep it a secret forever," I say.

Callie sets down the notepad, and Meatball starts chewing on it. "Okay, but I thought part of the point of going to a women's college was to just blend in, you know?"

I walk over to Queen Elizardbeth's cage, partly so she doesn't feel left out and partly for time to think about my answer. Liza follows me with her hazel eyes as I pick up her misting bottle. I spray her, and she closes her eyelids in sweet, moisturized bliss as the water droplets accumulate on her scales.

Finally, I say to Callie, "Being trans is who I am. I'll want to share that with people I'm close with, eventually." At least, I *hope* I will. I'm, like, ninety-seven-point-five percent sure that @thesp_ian will still want to be friends when he finds out I'm trans. Sometimes he goes to Botetourt parties with the theater folks, and he talks about how queer-friendly everyone is.

"Well. If anyone tries to start a fiery riot, I'll . . ." Callie flounders. Then she starts tearing up and sniffling.

"*Cal.* I'm going to be fine."

She shakes her head. "It's not that." *Sniff sniff.* Meatball starts licking her face again, in tune with her change in mood. "I was just thinking about Meatball having a really bad seizure, and me being too far away to say goodbye. And then the last time I see him is at the funeral, where I'll be expected to keep it together when all I want to do is fall apart." She is fully sobbing.

"*Cal.*"

"No one else loves him like I do!" she wails.

Meatball lets out a tiny bark.

"Cal, you don't have to apply if you don't want to."

Callie wipes her eyes and blows her nose. "I am not emotionally capable of having this conversation right now," she says.

As she sniffles, my phone rings. Mr. Walker's photo fills the screen—the picture I snapped on Halloween last year when he dressed up as one of the witches from *Macbeth*.

"Hello?" I say tentatively. My armpits drip like I've just sprayed *them* with a misting bottle. Mr. Walker texts rehearsal updates sometimes, but he's never called me on a Saturday.

"Hi, Lucy, it's Mr. Walker. Do you have a minute?"

Callie must notice my wide eyes, because she goes quiet. I put the phone on speaker. "Yep," I say. "And Callie's here, too."

"Great," Mr. Walker says. "That means I only have to deliver bad news once."

Shit sauce.

He lets out a breath. "Principal Schmidt will be sending a formal email, but the short of it is they're not allowing the play to move forward."

My mouth goes dry, my tongue turning to dust.

Sure, we knew School Board Karen was probably going to ban our flyer after she watched two teenagers pretend to get drunk onstage and ramble about gender-neutral pronouns. But they're banning the *show*? What is this, the McCarthy era?

"What!" Callie yells. Meatball leaps off her lap as she stands up. "Because the characters are trans?"

"It's absolute bullshit, pardon my French," Mr. Walker says. I've never heard him curse. "I think the school board is trying to avoid controversy, but this is a step too far."

I'm too stunned and angry to say anything, but this news has the opposite effect on Callie. "In the original," she sputters, "Caliban literally tries to rape Miranda every chance he gets. Would the school board prefer we perform *that* version?"

"I know this is disappointing, girls."

"Maybe we should've added a book-burning bonfire," Callie continues. "That would've been the school board's wet dream."

Mr. Walker pauses to make sure she's finished. "They're giving you the option to revise the show, if you're willing. They want you to remove the content about Miranda being trans and Ariel being nonbinary."

"Oh, so rewrite the whole thing?" Callie explodes. "Yeah, no problem. Let me and Lucy just type that up quick."

I try to find words, but the anger just presses on my chest, suffocating me. Finally I manage, "But Ariel *is* nonbinary in the original. Their gender is never specified."

"I'm truly sorry this is happening." Mr. Walker sounds exhausted and pissed. "If you decide to cancel the show, you'll still get an A on the assignment. It's a great play, and you should be proud of it."

Callie and I look at each other, stunned. *Cancel?*

When Callie opens her mouth, I'm sure she's going to say what I'm thinking: *This was supposed to be Lucy's stage debut as a woman.* But she doesn't.

"But it's our Hughes audition," Callie says, exasperated. "It *has* to go up."

Right. Hughes. A judge is scheduled to come watch our showcase, as part of our application process. No showcase, no Hughes audition.

Mr. Walker sighs like he's about to tell us our grandmothers died. "Unfortunately, you would forfeit your chance at Hughes."

I don't meet Callie's gaze in case I start crying.

"So either we rewrite the script or we give up on Hughes," Callie says flatly. "That's what they're telling us?"

"You'd still have the option to do general studies at Central next year and join Hughes as a sophomore," Mr. Walker says without a hint of enthusiasm. That's Carina and Deja's plan. But from what I've read, Hughes only takes a few sophomores each year. Getting in would be even more of a crapshoot than it already is.

"I know that's not the news you were hoping for," Mr. Walker continues. "And, girls? If you decide to fight back, I'm behind you. But it's your choice."

When I end the call, Callie collapses onto her bed. "Fu-u-u-uck," she wails.

I grasp the wire of Liza's cage, letting her iridescent scales lure my brain away from the deep, despondent pit it wants to collapse into.

We should call a press conference, or record an angry video, or recruit our friends to picket outside the school district building. I *want to* want to do those things.

But I'm exhausted.

6

BACK AT HOME, I POWER UP MY
Xbox to let the day's trauma melt from my brain.
My friend Alex is online, which is perfect: she
knows zero details about the school board drama
but about five thousand and one details about my new
friendship with @thesp_ian.

"It's just a few messages back and forth," I say into
my crappy mic as we search for diamonds in *Minecraft,* our
favorite comfort game. We both know it's more like a few hundred messages at this point. But that sounds creepy to say out loud
about a friend I've never met IRL who happens to be a dude.

"Yeah, a few messages back and forth with a major hottie who
shares your passion for the theater." She pronounces the last word
thee-uh-tuh. Alex lives in San Diego. She's a tall, eleven-out-of-ten
Puerto Rican goddess with legs that won't quit (IRL, not in the
game), so she's not exactly in tune with my romantic prospects.

Even though Callie is my best friend, I haven't been able to tell her about him. I'm just worried she'll think I have a crush on him or something, and that's why I want to visit Botetourt. Which I don't, and it isn't. So it feels good to talk about Ian with Alex. Plus she's trans too. So besides online videos and random blogs, she's where I turn with my questions, sob sessions, and gripes.

Alex would one hundred percent want to know about the school board thing, but I can't bring myself to mention it. She'd probably vent her fury on the internet, harnessing the outrage of all her friends, family, and followers. But I just want the whole thing to go away.

"I don't ooze the beauty and charisma that makes boys fall for me immediately," I say. "Like some women I know." Alex laughs but doesn't deny it. I pull my knees into my chest. "But for real. I'm just excited to have a friend whose mom works there. That would, like, never happen at Central."

"Well, I do love a friends-to-lovers storyline," Alex says suggestively.

I roll my eyes and blast a creeper to smithereens.

"Now let's talk outfits," Alex says.

I tell her about the clothes I picked out—she's psyched for the warrior princess dress—and she gives me tips for glamming up my hair and makeup. My makeup case lies splayed open on my dresser, full of drugstore mascara and chalky eye shadow. I don't even own the highlighter and bronzer she's talking about. "Can you just come on the visit with me?" I beg.

She laughs. "If that means I get a taste of Sweet Babycakes while I'm there, I might take you up on that."

"You can have him!" I laugh. "As long as you make yourself available to be my personal how-to-girl coach."

Alex cracks up. "Shut up. You're beautiful and sweet and *you are a girl*. Just do what I do. Purse your lips, bat your eyelashes, and pop your booty out a little bit. Works like a charm."

"I don't *have* a booty."

"You don't need a *physical* booty. You just need to harness that spiritual-booty energy."

I roll my eyes. "I'll get right on that. But can you at least fly out to do my makeup? I'll pay you in complimentary waffles from the dining hall."

My phone pings, but I ignore it, keeping my focus on the game.

Alex laughs. "I'll send you a good video. Right after I slash this mob of Slenderman-looking motherfuckers."

After we've cleared that section of cave, I peek at my phone.

> **@thesp_ian:** Hey friend.
> How ya doin tonight?

Oh my goddess.

"Sorry, gotta go, Alex," I say, and throw the controller on the floor.

"Say hi to Babycakes for me," she calls as I take off the headset.

I type, Shitty day, but better now.

> **@thesp_ian:** What happened?

Shit. Of course, he has no idea about the showcase. And he has no idea I'm facing transphobia, because he has no idea I'm trans. Keeping up an internet facade is a full-time job.

I take a deep breath. Maybe I can give him a tiny morsel of information about what's going on. Just as a test.

@lucygoosey: The school is trying to shut down this play I'm part of

@thesp_ian: Oooh, sounds scandalous. Is there a nude scene or something?

I take one more deep breath before responding.

@lucygoosey: Ha. Not even. It's just got some trans characters in it, and the school thinks people are gonna flip their shit. They forbade us from performing it onstage

My hands tremble as I wait for his response.

@thesp_ian: WTF??? They are out of their MINDS

@thesp_ian: No wonder you want to get out of that school. What year is it there, 1952?

My shoulders relax. Then I laugh. Why did I ever worry Ian would be weird about me being trans?

○ ○ ○

THE NEXT AFTERNOON, CALLIE AND I MEET AT work to get some extra hours. If we have to discuss how to resist the forces of an oppressive regime, at least we can do it on the clock. I take the wet wheel this time, and soon my hands are covered in cold, wet pumice.

"So the question is whether to revise the play to appease the transphobes," Callie begins, firing up the dry wheel. She raises her voice over the whir of the machines. "*Or* conjure a hurricane to blow down the school district building, killing everyone inside."

"*Cal.*" I roll my eyes.

"Fine. Inconveniencing everyone inside by making them cold and wet."

I finish polishing a clear, glittery retainer and hand it to her. "To be honest, I have no idea what we should do." My brain is churning with anger, but my exhausted body is wilting like old lettuce. I tick off all the responsibilities on my plate: finishing (or starting) my college applications, planning a weekend road trip to a school six hours away, and maintaining a friendship with an internet man whose mom teaches at my dream school. Not to mention directing and starring in a play.

Callie leans toward her work, concentrating on bringing out the retainer's shine. "Well, I looked up how to call a press conference, and it said Tuesdays through Thursdays at ten a.m. gets the most viewership for some reason."

A viral news story doesn't exactly help with the "fresh start" I'm looking for. "What if we protest and petition and all that, but they *still* ban our show?" I sigh. "We pushed back on the flyer, and that just made things worse."

Callie nods, staring off into the distance with an absent gaze as she presses the retainer into the polishing wheel. She's about to shine that thing into a hand mirror.

"Callie!"

She jumps and pulls the retainer away. "Sorry! I was just thinking about how we could revise the show and still make it, you know, good."

I choose an ugly orange-and-black upper expander, which the kid probably chose the colors for on Halloween. "You know? If the school board demands that I play a cis woman in the show, that's revolutionary in its own way, right?" But as I say it, guilt festers in my belly. Step by step, we're convincing ourselves that the school board's demands aren't that bad.

Callie nods. "Right."

"And Miranda could still struggle against her controlling father," I say. "She doesn't *have* to be trans." I'm a literal troll right now. Report me for harassment.

"Totally," Callie says. "And that way, you for sure get to have your theatrical debut as a woman."

"And we'll get to put on a kick-ass Hughes audition," I add.

Callie raises an eyebrow. "You still care about that?"

"*Yes,*" I say. And I mean it. "It's been our Dream for forever. If I don't go to Central, I want it to be because my audition sucks, or because I visited a different school and fell in love with it. Not because some School Board Karen's butthole is clenched so tight a fart can't even slip out."

Callie laughs, but her eyes look sad. "But this feels bad, right?"

My shoulders deflate. "It feels horrible. Like we're letting down trans people everywhere." Alex would be so disappointed in me.

Both of us take a deep breath. I study Callie's face to guess what's going through her head, and she does the same to me. As far as I can tell, we're both torn: we want to fight back, but we don't want to fuck up our audition.

Finally, Callie says, "Well, we could perform the real version of our play next year, right? We could spend the summer making it even gayer."

"Hughes students don't get to direct real shows until they're seniors," I remind her, and her face falls. "But maybe we could do it in the cafeteria or something?" I suggest.

After I pass the final retainer to Callie, I scrape cold, goopy pumice from my hands. In the sink, the scalding-hot water rinses my skin clean, and the gray mush swirls down the drain. *There go my convictions.*

7

WHEN THE NIGHT BEFORE OUR trip finally arrives, Mom and Dad buzz around me like horseflies.

"Toothbrush and toothpaste?" Dad asks. As if *he's* the one who works in the dental hygiene and alignment industry.

"Dad, this isn't sleepaway camp," I say.

They still think Callie and I are just driving an hour away to Central. I *know* it's wrong to go on this trip without telling them. But listen: there's no way in a trillion years that my parents would agree to the two of us driving my janky-ass car three hundred miles away. On a school day. And *not* going isn't an option.

"I still don't like the idea of you missing Friday classes. Did you and Callie get your revision turned in?" Mom asks.

The school board gave us a deadline of tonight, with the promise that they'll read and approve it by tomorrow, so we can jump straight into rehearsals again on Monday. Callie and I canceled rehearsals and spent the last week and a half revising. Hopefully the "vacation" will placate our cast when we ask them to memorize a whole new script.

"We're sending it tonight," I say. I just have a few more awkward transitions to smooth out, and then I'll send it. Callie thought it was ready to go three days ago, but she's letting me do my perfectionist thing.

Mom sighs. "I don't see why you girls can't just drive up after school ends."

Obviously because we need to spend the entire day driving to make it to Botetourt's check-in time at five p.m. But we have an answer for this. "It's so we can sit in on classes. We get to visit Intro to Acting and a lighting class."

Mom smiles. "That *is* pretty cool."

Guilt tightens around my neck—both for lying to Mom and for sneaking off to a school so far away. If her cancer came back—goddess forbid—it'd take me half a day to get home.

But Dad has his lips squished to one side. *Does he know?* I wonder. Maybe he checked the search history on my laptop and found all my visits to Botetourt's website.

But then he asks, "What are you wearing for the drive?"

I relax, rolling my eyes. He just wants to play fashion police. "Dad. I don't know."

"Why does that matter?" Mom asks him.

"Because if she gets pulled over and her license doesn't match her"—he waves a hand in front of his face—"getup, I'm worried about what might happen."

Dad loves to whip out his ally training when he thinks he's

protecting me from danger. But when it comes to the fun stuff—embracing my name, my style, my pronouns—he's more of a Prospero.

I take a deep breath. "Callie will be there. We'll be safe. It's just Central."

"Which outfit did you choose for your admissions meeting?" Mom asks cheerily, trying to change the subject.

"The green dress." The forest-nymph outfit turned out super cute and totally professional, as long as I wear tights. And don't bend down too seductively if I drop a pencil on the floor. Not that I've been practicing. I've got it down so that I look sexy as hell, but there's no chance of flashing my stuffed A cups. (Mom and I both agree that socks are cheaper and comfier than silicone inserts.)

"Did you pack your makeup kit?"

"Mom, yes," I say, exasperated. She's going to try to talk me into going light on the makeup.

Mom pulls a tube of lipstick from her pocket and hands it to me. "Then maybe you can keep this one in your purse."

The color is called Sweet Success. A good omen. I wrap Mom in a tight hug, and she squeezes me back like one of the stress toys with the eyes that pop out.

Dad freezes up during this exchange but creaks to life to hand me what looks like a hot-pink asthma inhaler. "Keep this on your keychain. It's mace. I don't know what kind of people you'll run into." He can't meet my eye.

"You're two girls traveling alone," Mom adds. "This will help you protect yourselves, just in case."

But I know Dad isn't just worried about us being girls. He's worried about me being *me*.

Before I go to bed, I give the script a final once-over. A sick feeling rumbles in my gut. There's not a speck of trans-girl magic in this new version. It's sanitized and generic, just like the school board asked for.

Maybe we should've fought back after all.

But it's too late now. I save the document, attach it to an email, and hit send.

"Fuck you, fuckers," I say, slamming the laptop shut.

IN THE MORNING, I THROW ON SOME COMFY

road-trip sweats and pull my hair into a small ponytail—which it's finally long enough for now. No makeup yet. If I *do* get pulled over—knock on wood—I'll look more like my driver's license. I open my wallet to double-check it's there, tucked in behind my KD's Frozen Custard reward card. I usually keep my license in the back, out of sight, but now I bring it to the front. I don't want to be stuck digging for it just in case we get pulled over. I shudder when I look at it, the deadname screaming up at me like a car alarm I can't shut off. And the picture is from two years ago, when I'd only been on hormones a few weeks. I hate the way I look, but it also makes me grateful to see how far I've come since then.

At Callie's, Asha lets me inside, tiny Meatball yapping at her feet.

"Hi, baby," I coo. Meatball flops onto his side, presenting his fuzzy beige belly for me to pet. "Who's a good boy?" He hops up and sticks his nose straight into my crotch for a deep sniff. "Okay, that's enough." I divert his attention by dangling my keys in front of his face.

On the couch, twelve-year-old Nikhil sits by the window with his backpack on, playing his Nintendo Switch as he waits for the bus. "Meatball threw up twice today," he says without looking up. "So watch out."

"Thanks for the warning." I scratch Meatball under the chin, and his tail whirls like a helicopter propeller. "You seem fine now, baby," I say in my just-for-Meatball voice.

"Ah, there's Sleeping Beauty," Asha says, glancing toward the stairs.

"It's so-o-o-o-o early," Callie whines as she plods down. Her hoodie, pj pants, and messed-up hair—no, her messed-up everything—make the statement obvious. "I'm almost done packing. And I gotta feed Liza." She kisses Meatball, hugs me, then grabs a few green leaves from Asha's smoothie prep area and trudges back upstairs.

Asha offers me breakfast while Callie gets ready. "Breakfast" being the green sludge she's blending with the remaining greens, plus some grainy brown muffins on the table. Luckily, a pot of coffee steams in the coffeemaker. "I'll just take my usual," I say.

I pour myself a cup and nibble a muffin. Bran, without even any raisins. I roll it in a napkin while I pet Meatball under the table.

Callie comes back downstairs, still a mess but now holding a burrito-shaped duffel bag.

"Ready?" I ask, hopping up.

"I'm still dead, but yes." She empties the rest of the coffee pot into a massive thermos, and I down what's left in my mug. "You're the man of the house now, Meatball." Callie picks him up and smooches him on the forehead. "Oooh, Mama's going to miss you so, so much. Don't you change a bit while I'm gone." He licks her face. Which is the closest thing to a shower she's getting today.

In the car, we wave goodbye to Asha until she's out of sight, at which point Callie pulls a bottle of chocolate syrup from her duffel.

"So much better," Callie mutters sleepily as she squirts syrup into the thermos and shakes it up. Asha doesn't approve of processed sugar, especially before nine a.m. "Hey, you sent in the revision, right?"

"Yep." I nod. "I gave you back a line from the original: 'Hell is empty, and all the devils are here.' Hope that's okay."

Callie chuckles. "Nice. I'll find out where School Board Karen is sitting and say it directly to her."

We pass the chocolatey caffeine bomb back and forth, and Callie cues up the "Super Awesome Road-Trip Mix!!!!!" playlist we've been working on between revision sessions. "Everything Is Awesome" by Tegan and Sara blasts from the speakers.

"Everything is Luce-eyyyyyyy," Callie belts. This jam became our theme song when I first told Callie my chosen name. She needed a way to get used to saying it, so she incorporated it into every song she heard, ever. "Everything is loose when you're Lucy Goosey." Actually, that's what inspired my social media handle: @lucygoosey.

Callie's superpower is that she can just roll with the punches. Oh, you're gay, seventh-grade best friend? Great. Love it. Oh, wait, you're actually trans, ninth-grade bestie? Thanks for telling me.

Wow, senior-in-high-school Lucy, you're applying to a different school and throwing our Dream down the drain? Let me plan a road trip to help with that.

At a stoplight, I type out a message to Ian: On our way south! We were up late last night, messaging back and forth about the trip.

"Stay alive, don't text and drive," Callie says, reaching for my phone. "I can text your mom for you."

I plunge the phone into the car door pocket. "That's okay. It can wait."

Not telling Callie about Ian feels like trying to hold a melting scoop of ice cream behind my back. I fell in love with Botetourt before I even knew Ian existed. But what if Callie thinks I'm abandoning the Dream for some boy? He's not even a branch on my decision tree.

He's just a leaf, who happens to be on the branch. A particularly handsome leaf, who, I admit, I might have the teeniest, tiniest crush on.

"Breakfast?" I ask, changing the subject with a bag of sour gummy worms from the center console.

We have six hours of super jammable music but only about six minutes' worth of gummy worms. So after a few hours of singing and dancing in her seat, Callie changes some lyrics to "I'm so-o-o-o-o hungry!" Our stomachs rumble like two thunderclouds colliding.

We both see the sign at the same time. "Grandpa's Cheese Barn!" we yell.

Callie shrieks, "We have to go!"

I pull off, following the signs for the cheese Mecca.

Some sort of road-trip recklessness comes over us, and we

splurge on a sit-down meal. Our waitress is wearing a cheese-patterned shirt and a name tag that says *Her Majestcheese: Jennifer.*

"I'll try the Gouda Time Burger," Callie tells her. "Your Majest-cheese," she adds.

The waitress laughs dryly and frowns.

I hum a note to make sure my register reads "socially accept-able girl" before ordering the Cheddar Than Homemade Mac 'n' Cheese. My road-trip sweatpants and makeup-free face don't exactly scream femininity. Neither do Callie's, but she's got that sweet, sweet cis privilege.

"I'll have that right up for you guys," the waitress says without giving me a second look. Success.

"God, if I ever get to the point in life where cheese-themed sur-roundings make me visibly irritated, it's time for an intervention." Callie shakes her head at the waitress as she disappears into the kitchen. "She doesn't know how good she has it."

"She probably makes, like, five bucks an hour."

"You can't put a price on life in a cheese sanctuary!" Callie pounds her fist on the table. "'Tis a *holy* place."

Her Majestcheese Jennifer returns to collect empty plates from the table next to us, where three old ladies with gray cotton candy haircuts sit. "Anything else I can getcha, ladies?"

Ladies. She called me and Callie *guys.*

While we wait, we color Grandpa and his cows on our place-mats because we're both eight years old. I help a cow navigate a maze to reach the rest of her herd. Poor cow, getting left behind.

"Why was the cow so sad?" Callie asks, reading from a list of jokes on a table tent.

"Hmm. Postpartum depression?" I guess.

"What? That's not even clever."

I look at her seriously. "Cow depression is no laughing matter."

"You could've said it postpar-*dung* depression, at least."

"You joke, when poor Bessie can't even afford her Zoloft from the *farm*-acy." I take the table tent and read the real answer to her joke. "She was making *blue* cheese?" I look up at her, confused. "That's the stupidest shit I've ever heard."

Callie snorts, her lip quivers, and a spray of Mountain Dew erupts from her mouth. I shield my face and burst out laughing. She falls over in her chair, dying.

The table of Golden Girls glares at us. "People are staring," I say.

"Sheesh. Some people just don't appreciate a good cheese joke. How stuck up can you Brie?"

After we finish our food, Her Majestcheese sets a black bill book on the table. Directly in front of me. Inside, the receipt lists both of our meals and drinks.

I'm about to ask to split the bill when she says, "Whenever you're ready, sir," and walks away.

I freeze with the book in my hand. The mac 'n' cheese congeals into a brick in my stomach. The words on the receipt shudder in front of me—my hand is shaking.

"Luce," Callie says, worry wavering in her voice. "Fuck her." She reaches across the table and squeezes my hand in hers. "She made it clear she hates happiness, anyway."

No tears are coming, thank goddess. But hot shame warms up my cheeks. Did the waitress want to hurt me on purpose? She probably doesn't see many trans people come through, out here in the middle of nowhere.

Or worse. Did the thought never cross her mind that I could be a woman?

I push the dysphoria deep, deep down, like I'm burying a dead goldfish in the dirt.

"It's okay," I mutter, and slip a twenty into the book. Callie adds the rest, and we get up before the waitress returns.

We wander next door to ye olde cheese shoppe and browse a refrigerated case with hundreds of different cheeses. Massive wheels of dairy that I never believed existed in real life until right now. It's a miracle. More rare than a double rainbow. I force myself to appreciate it instead of wasting brain space on Her Majestbitch Jennibutt.

"We have to get some cheese for the road, right?" I say. Fuck the budget. I need an emotional-support road-trip snack. Besides, my parents did send along a little money. They thought it was for a one-hour trip to Central, but still.

"Sounds Gouda," Callie says. She runs her finger along a row of off-brand gummy candies priced by weight. "And maybe some marshmallow-belly frogs?"

"Naturally." I hug a sliver of sharp cheddar to my chest: $3.62.

"Mmm. Circusy," Callie says after a big inhale of disgusting orange circus peanuts. I push her hand back before she can grab another.

"Not even circus peanuts deserve your nose germs."

She opens her mouth, probably to defend the honor of her boogers, but stops when she looks past me and gasps. I turn to face a wall of jugs—gold, pink, and dark purple.

I take a closer look at the labels. "What's blueberry cider?" I ask.

Callie stares at the nutrition facts. "Water, blueberries, apples, unicorn orgasms. Where have you been all my life?"

I've never seen someone so excited about juice. "Get it."

"But it's sixteen dollars."

I shrug. "Okay, then don't get it."

"But it looks so wholesome and delicious," she says while cradling the jug like a baby. "Why did I put in all those hours of sweat and tears at the orthodontist's, if not to provide and care for this precious infant?"

"What are we even going to do with an entire gallon of cider? What if our dorm room doesn't have a fridge?"

"Why would we need a fridge?" She raises an eyebrow.

"Callie, not even we can drink all that—"

"Are you challenging me, girl?" she yells. "Are *you* challenging *me*? I'll show you. I'll show all the nonbelievers!" She shakes her fist in the air as she carries the jug to the cash register.

I adore her.

Behind the building, we walk along the fence that separates us from dozens of cows. I finger the cheddar wedge in my pocket like a worry stone.

"Look at the little one! She's so-o-o-o-o awkward!" Callie points to a calf hiding behind a larger cow. Her legs are super wobbly, and she lets out the most adorable noises. She's trying to cheer me up. And I'm trying to let her.

We stick some coins in a feeding machine and hold handfuls of brown pellets through the fence. (They bear a striking resemblance to Asha's bran muffins.) I make bleating sounds to attract the calf, but I sound more like a goat than a cow. Still, it's better than Callie's attempt. . . .

"MOO! MOO! MOO!" she yells. She flaps her arms like they're chicken wings for some reason.

I snort and start laughing. I can't help it.

"Remember that time I was working sound board and accidentally played a warthog fart instead of a gunshot?" Callie asks.

I laugh harder. "What the hell does that have to do with anything?"

"Nothing, I just know it always makes you laugh."

And just like that, I feel better.

Something warm and wet touches my hand, and I yelp. The mama cow's tongue is slobbering all over my palm as she laps up the pellets.

"Hello, mama," Callie coos.

Then the calf is here at the fence. I move my hand to offer her pellets, too. "Hello, awkward little one," I say, and she takes a tentative lick. "You and I have a lot in common."

Even after being me full-time since last year, I'm still trying to find my legs. Is it obvious to everyone else?

8

A FEW HOURS LATER, THE LAND-
scape has transformed from flat, yellow-brown
fields to rolling hills, to mountains crowded with
orange-and-brown trees. I've never been to this part
of the country, but it feels familiar.

Familiar, like this driver's seat. On which my ass
went numb an hour ago.

Callie takes another pull of the cider, which is now down
to just a few inches of cloudy swill at the bottom of the jug. She
swipes a hand across her lips and says in a Western cowboy drawl,
"Ain't never seen nothin' as purty as these here parts."

"Darn tootin'," I say, slipping into the same accent. "And I ain't
never seen a dame as purty as this'n here order a jug o' the devil's
iced tea and warsh the entirety down'r gullet."

Callie laughs so hard she spews a little cider onto the dashboard. She really needs to work on mouth control. "Where'd you
learn that voice?"

I shrug. *Red Dead Redemption*. Callie's never played the video game, but she nods like she knows what I'm talking about.

We crest a hill, and a valley of reds and oranges opens in front of us. The town of little houses is flanked by mountains on three sides, and the trees outnumber buildings about a hundred to one. "Oh my god, Luce." Callie's eyes widen.

"Yeah," I say. Cue the twinkling harp music. It's like a postcard for autumn leaves.

Callie tilts her head back, chugs the last few swallows of cider, and smacks her lips together. "Challenge. Complete."

I tip my invisible cowboy hat to her. "Boy howdy, pardna."

I know Callie made up this cider "challenge" to cheer me up after the waitress thing. And it's working. I'm not going to let one comment from one grumpy rando derail my weekend. But we *are* going to stop at a gas station so I don't show up to campus looking like I rolled out of the Goodwill donation bin. Plus Callie's about to burst like a fire hydrant.

At a Shell station, Callie pees and I change into a slouchy gray sweater, leggings, and boots. There's no room to spread out my makeup supplies, so I keep it simple with concealer, light foundation, mascara, and tinted lip balm. I scrutinize myself in the mirror. *Deep breath.*

"Do I look okay?" I ask Callie.

Callie smiles and squeezes me. "You look amazing."

But of course, she always says that. I add a touch more foundation to my jawline. No matter how recently I've shaved, a few spots of stubble always manage to poke through.

"You ready?" Callie asks.

I stare her straight in the eye, take a deep breath, and say, "Darn tootin'."

FROM THE MAIN ROAD, BOTETOURT COLLEGE

is just an engraved sign standing between two pillars. The whole area is cloaked in grassy slopes, trees, and mystery. But as soon as we pull onto campus, buildings rise up like we're driving through an intricate pop-up book—red bricks, white pillars, sprawling wooden porches. As we walk up the stone steps to the student center, I smooth my hair and clear my throat.

"You've got this," Callie whispers, squeezing my hand.

We step through a blue-and-yellow balloon arch, and a mob of women in baby-blue polos bombards us with smiles, pamphlets, and branded cloth bags. "Welcome to Botetourt!" they say, over and over. So. Many. People.

I plaster a grin on my own face, hoping it doesn't look like a grimace. "Hi. Hi. Good, thanks. Hello. Drove down today. Pennsylvania," I say.

At the check-in table, I say "Lucy Myers" loudly and clearly. No question mark at the end. No room for anyone to mishear it as "Lewis" or "Levi." Like I've been saying this name my whole life. The woman smiles, passes me my name tag, and hands me a marker to add my pronouns. I write *she/her* in thick, confident letters.

"Okay, I love the pronouns," Callie whispers to me as she writes *she/her* under her name. "But isn't *everybody* a she/her at a women's college?"

I shrug. "Some people might use they/them or they/she, you know?" I'm just relieved I'm not the only one they asked for pronouns. Which is what usually happens.

A student with short hair brushed forward like 2009 Justin Bieber guides us into a dining hall. "Hi, ladies. I'll let y'all's hosts know that you're here. Looks like you'll be staying in Calvin Hall."

The *ladies* sends a shiver up my spine. And can we get a round of applause for the word *y'all*? It's the perfect pronoun: informal, gender-neutral, and warm like fresh peach cobbler.

When the student is out of earshot, Callie waggles her eyebrows at me. "There's so many gay people here!" she whispers.

For a straight girl, she has great gaydar. I give her a don't-be-so-obvious look. But she's right. I haven't seen such a high concentration of beanies and Doc Martens since the *Rocky Horror* show Callie and I went to at the Finnegan Theater in Pittsburgh. Good sign.

Callie and I dig through our heavy goodie bags: pamphlets, course catalog, map, pens, magnet, drink koozie, chip clip, and a million coupons for businesses in town. I crack open the course catalog and flip to the Theater Arts section. Acting, Stagecraft, Costumecraft, Directing, Principles of Theatrical Design, Playwriting, Diverse Representation on Stage and Screen, Theater of Social Change . . . the list goes on. There's an entire concentration in Direction and Management. *Fuck yeah.*

"Damn, Cal, look at this list." This school may be small, but they don't fuck around with the course offerings.

But all of a sudden, Callie's head is in her lap. "Ughhh," she moans.

"What's wrong?"

She takes a few deep breaths, then sits up. "Okay. Wow. Crisis averted." Her forehead glistens with sweat.

"Um, what?" I rub her back in slow circles.

"Just a minor gut surge." She shrugs.

"No. That is not a thing. What happened?"

"Luce, I'm *fine*." Her stomach gurgles so boisterously that the girl and her mom next to us turn to look.

"Is it the cider?" I whisper.

"Maybe." Another shrug.

"I *told* you not to drink that whole thing. Go to the bathroom!"

"I'm fine now, okay?" She pulls her own course catalog from her tote. "I want to see the theater classes."

We look through the course descriptions together, and I can tell Callie is surprised at how many options there are. "Stage Combat One?" she shouts. "That implies the existence of"—she turns the page—"Stage Combat Two? Holy shit, Luce, screw the acting major. I'm studying stage stabbing."

I smile. This is a good start.

A middle-aged woman in an oversized blue-and-yellow top hat has arrived, and she's walking around to shake hands. "So happy you joined us this weekend!" Her voice fills up the room like hot air in a blimp. Parents put hands on their students' backs to push them toward her.

"Is she the headmaster or something?" Callie whispers.

"This isn't a British boarding school," I whisper back. But what do I know? "She'd be head*mistress*, anyway."

When she finally makes her way to our side of the room, I stand up, smoothing my hair again.

"Hello. I'm Sandy, dean of students," she says, and grips my hand like one of us is falling off a cliff. "Where are you visiting from this weekend?" Her name tag says *Sandy Sanchez, Dean of Students*. She hasn't added pronouns.

I flash a stage smile. "Lucy Myers," I say. "Pennsylvania."

"Quite a drive!" she booms. "I'm originally a northeasterner myself. Upstate New York. But I've been here at Botetourt for thirty years now. Don't do the math on that one." And she tips her head back and laughs at her joke. She's corny but warm. The top hat suits her.

She's shaking Callie's hand, but Callie's face is ghost white.

"And this is Callie," I add quickly. "Also from Pennsylvania." *What's wrong?* I plead with my eyes. It's not like her to clam up in a social setting. That's *my* prerogative. But Callie widens her eyes at me. Sweat glistens on her forehead, and her lips wither into a thin, straight line.

Sandy must be used to shy high school students, because she doesn't bat an eye. "We're so glad you're here," she says. "What are you most looking forward to this weekend?"

"I can't wait to see the theater," I say. "We're both interested in the drama program. Directing for me, acting for Callie." Acting like a sweaty marble statue, anyway.

Sandy's face lights up. "*I* was a theater major! That was years ago, of course." Another laugh echoes off the walls. "Oh, you'll love the program here. Absolutely stellar faculty. And the theater building? Just gorgeous. A lot of love went into that space. You'll have to check out the show tomorrow night! It's a dress rehearsal, but all prospective students are invited. It's going to be really special."

91

"That's awesome," I say, not even trying to keep my smile under control. "And I saw on the website that you have quite a few student-run shows every year?"

"Abso*lutely*. In fact"—she scans the room and points to a student in an emerald jumpsuit—"the head of our theater society is just over there. Frida. Can I introduce you?"

Right now? "That'd be amazing," I say.

"Ms. Dean," Callie interrupts, "could you actually point us toward the restroom?"

Us? And it's Ms. *Sanchez*, not Ms. Dean. She *is* the dean. Or maybe it's even *Dr.*, which makes this even more embarrassing.

"Um, it's right down that hallway, dear," she says, pointing.

Callie locks eyes with me, and her expression screams, *I need help.*

My face yells back, *Can you please handle this one on your own, because I'm a little busy?*

An enormous rumble gurgles from her belly. Callie gazes into my soul and imprints a message directly in my brain: *I swear on the life of Meatball that I cannot survive this upcoming hurdle without the support of my best friend.*

Okay. I take a breath. "I'm so sorry, Dean Sanchez. Could I take you up on that offer in a couple minutes?" Callie is already tugging me along behind her. Sandy gives me a confused frown and then pivots to greet the next group of students. *Fuck.*

Callie slams a stall door shut behind her, and Mount Vesuvius erupts. "Ughhhhhhhh," she groans. "I'm giving birth."

"What the fuck, Cal." I slide into the stall next to hers. I consider reaching under the partition to hold her hand, but that's a little too far, even for us. So I pull up a meme of one puppy telling another "You can do it!" and hold out my phone near her feet. She reaches down and makes a heart shape with her hands.

"I told you that cider was a bad idea," I say.

"Yes, but"—a plopping waterfall interrupts the sentence—"I didn't listen to you." Her voice is strained and miserable. "Ughhh, I started pooping while we were talking to that top hat lady."

"Jesus Christ, Cal." I gag.

A stall door slams shut and quick footsteps flee the scene. Smart move.

I bury my face inside my sweater and whisper reassurances through it. I clench my eyes shut against the stinging air. My sinuses burn like I just swallowed a glob of wasabi.

Still, I manage to pound out a message to @thesp_ian. We made it! You busy tonight?

Callie sighs loudly and starts unrolling the toilet paper. The eruption has passed.

"You feel better, Cal?" I ask.

She replies breathlessly, "Yes. But I need—" She hesitates.

"What do you need?"

"Clean underwear."

I slip out of the bathroom and run to the car like I'm absconding from a crime scene. Callie and her antics. Sometimes they're funny, but right now I feel like I've brought a middle schooler on a business trip.

This is not the first impression I was going for.

OUR HOSTS ARE TWO FRESHMEN—EXCUSE
me, *first years,* because this is not a *men's* school. Zuri is an international student from Ethiopia. And Reena is an American student who was born in India. "We moved to D.C. when I was five," she clarifies. She and Callie immediately start fangirling over their favorite Bollywood movies. Callie must've purged all the cider from her system, because she's back to her usual self.

Calvin Hall is old and grand, with lofty ceilings, formidable wooden staircases that creak with each step, and floors that are just slightly lopsided. Zuri and Reena's room has two big windows overlooking the quad. Twin beds are pushed against opposite walls, one side of the room decorated with dozens of Polaroids and the other crowded with potted houseplants and tiny cacti. A string of white Christmas lights hangs above the windows, stretching from one bed to the other.

"This is awesome," I say, leaning over the bed for a closer look at the photos. They're artsy shots: a lamppost with a soft glow, two clasped hands, a girl mid-laugh. I picture my own imaginary dorm room: playbills from my favorite shows, signed film posters, and an antique velvet armchair.

"So give us the scoop," Callie says, rolling out her sleeping bag. "What's it like going to a school in the forest with no boys?"

Reena laughs. "Um, awesome? I've made so many friends"—she smiles at Zuri—"and my classes are all really interesting. And classroom discussions with women are just"—she kisses her fingertips—"perfect. It sounds cheesy, but I swear they're not paying us to say this."

"I really like it, too," Zuri adds. She sits on her wooden desk chair backward, like a cool next-door neighbor I never knew I needed. "I wanted a really small school. That felt safer, since I was coming from so far away."

Three hundred miles doesn't feel far at all, compared to a sixteen-hour flight.

"So do you know, like, everyone here?" I ask.

"Not by name," Reena says. "But I've probably seen everybody around at one point or another."

"Dean Sanchez was going to introduce us to this girl named Frida. She's the head of the theater society? But then we didn't get to meet her." Callie gives me an apologetic smile. Frida had left by the time we emerged from the stench sauna.

Zuri and Reena look at each other. "We don't know a lot of theater people," Zuri says.

"But I think I saw a show on the schedule for tomorrow?" Reena adds.

I pull out my bright yellow schedule.

Saturday 7 PM: Come see a dress rehearsal for *Party of Possum* by the Botetourt Theater Department. Intended for current and prospective students.

"That's so cool, Luce," Callie says. "Maybe she'll be there."

I nod. "Yeah, maybe," I say. "Even if she's not, it'll be great to see a show." It's not Callie's fault her butt exploded at an inopportune moment. Well, it kind of is. But still. I cross my eyes at Callie to let her know I'm not mad.

95

"Okay, but be real with us." Callie cracks her knuckles and takes a deep breath. "How are the parties?"

Reena and Zuri laugh, obviously having expected a tougher question. "Okay, so—" "Well—" they say over each other.

"Listen," Reena says. "It depends where you go. The school-sponsored ones? They're pretty boring."

"But the Sheep parties?" Zuri says. "So much fun."

Oh goddess. Are we that far south that the parties happen in barns?

"Botetourt Arts Association. BAA," Reena clarifies. "It's where the dancers and painters and general cool kids live. But we just call it Sheep."

Callie and I grin at each other. "Sounds like our jam," Callie says.

"Oh, thank god," Reena laughs. "We were afraid we'd have to skip the one tonight to keep you company."

Excitement bubbles in my chest. A real. College. Party. I whip out my phone and read the new message from @thesp_ian. Nope, not busy. What did you have in mind?

I pound out my message: . . . Sheep party???

9

BEFORE THE REAL PARTY, WE HAVE
to make an appearance at the college-sponsored
mixer. The bright yellow schedule calls it a "foam
party," which sounds like it might involve bounc-
ing on squishy gymnastics mats. The description says
Wear your name tag!, which gives us an idea of the vibe.
But we get decked out anyway.

I finger the black warrior princess dress in my duffel
but chicken out. I don't know if I'm ready to make that kind of
entrance. And it's definitely too revealing for jumping around and
doing somersaults.

On her own, Callie would change in the middle of the room—
she doesn't care who sees her junk—but she comes with me to the
bathroom so I don't feel awkward. We slip into adjacent stalls, and
I slide out of my leggings, careful not to let anything touch the gray
tile floor.

"What do you think so far?" I ask.

"Okay, I got off to a bad start, but"—she grunts as she tugs off her jeans, one leg flapping under the stall divider—"the vibe is supercool."

"You don't think it's too small?"

"So far, no. It seems like a place where everyone just knows you, you know? Kinda cool. I feel like I could"—more grunting—"get elected to the student council or something. That'd never happen at Central."

I laugh. "President Callie, you've got my vote."

"Nah, president is too much. Who's the one who bangs the gavel and yells at people?"

"Sergeant at arms?"

"Yeah, that."

"You really are a director at heart," I say. My heart flutters at the thought of Callie actually falling in love with Botetourt and us being roommates together. With a different, random roommate, I might be doomed to a year of changing in clammy bathroom stalls, depending on whether we became close friends. But Callie's the one person I'm okay changing in front of.

"Oh gosh, Lucy! You look gorgeous!" Zuri yells when we return to the room. I opted for shimmery black leggings and a maroon sweater dress. Pretty much what I've been wearing all day, but a little tighter and flashier. Zuri scrutinizes me for a minute, then runs to her closet. "This would look perfect on you," she gushes. I slip my arms into the leather jacket, and my cool factor instantly shoots up.

"Thanks," I say, and twirl in the door mirror. I can't help smiling.

"I'm not done," she continues. "Did you bring makeup?"

I pass her my zippered pouch, which looks like an elementary school pencil case next to her multitiered beauty organizer. "Sit," she orders.

"Okay if I use this?" she asks, already spreading my own foundation across my cheek. Her brush is so sturdy and full. I hope she doesn't notice my drugstore brushes, crusty from hours of practice in my bathroom before I knew how to clean them. I study her strokes and try to memorize them.

She pauses at my chin, and I suck in a breath. Her face is so close to mine. Of course she's noticed my stubble. "I get hair on my chin, too," she admits, her voice sympathetic.

I let out a nervous laugh. "It sucks, right?"

"It sucks *so* hard. But I'm coming to love it. It doesn't make me less of a woman." She shoots me a winning smile and gets right back to business. "That's one reason I love my gender studies class. I never realized how much bullshit I went through just by being a woman."

"Are you doing a gender studies major?" I ask, trying not to sound too interested.

Reena laughs. "Zuri's currently majoring in *everything*."

"There's so much to choose from!" Zuri says. "Right now, I'm leaning toward history and sociology, but I might add a minor in math, gender studies, or printmaking."

"I might major in stage combat," Callie says. She changed into a teal T-shirt and slouchy jeans and is running her finger along the titles on the bookshelf. She's not much of a makeup person, except onstage.

By the time Zuri puts her brush down, my stubble is invisible and my smoky eye will probably asphyxiate anyone who sees me.

I add the final touch—the Sweet Success lipstick from Mom. It's a plum-magenta color that totally rounds out the look. I'm the closest to a magazine cover girl I've ever been.

When we're almost ready to go, Reena pulls a tall, clear bottle from a dresser drawer. "No pressure at all if y'all don't want to drink, but . . ." She trails off.

Thank fucking goddess. We didn't bring any booze or weed with us in case we got pulled over. But a shot is exactly the lubricant I need tonight.

"We would be honored to partake," Callie says, bowing.

Reena waggles her eyebrows conspiratorially. "Then let's get this party started." She twists off the cap, the spicy tang of booze hitting my nose, and fills two shot glasses.

I take the one shaped like a bear holding a Great Smoky Mountains sign, and Callie takes the one with Betty White's face. We look at each other, nod, and tip back the drink in one swallow. It tastes like pie set on fire.

Zuri and Reena take theirs, and Zuri shudders. "What flavor is that?" she asks, coughing.

"Cinnamon roll," Reena says, shrugging. "Sounded good at the time."

Callie does an arm-wave dance à la SpongeBob SquarePants. I wiggle my shoulders and feel the warmth pulse through my body. I'm so ready for this.

WE ARRIVE AT THE BACK QUAD FASHIONABLY

late, and the mixer is about as raging as a tea party. A portable dance floor lies in the grass, completely empty. A couple dozen people stand to the side, clutching snack plates against their chests like body armor. Techno beats blast from a set of speakers in the corner, but the DJ might as well be playing cricket sounds. No sign of gymnastics mats, foam or otherwise.

"Told you," Reena says, shaking her head. "The snacks are gonna slap, though, 'cause they're trying to impress y'all."

We load up our plates with crackers, cheese, fancy olives with pits, mini fruit tarts, stuffed dates, and bruschetta with honest-to-goddess smoked salmon on top. These snacks are no joke. Then we join the crowd of people watching the DJ's lights flash across the empty dance floor.

I slip into people-watching mode. Most of the prospective students and their hosts don't look like they changed from the clothes they had on earlier. There are a lot of girls with blond highlights and pearl earrings, but also several with short, funky haircuts. It seems like the kind of place where you can dress however you want to. A girl with short curls and a full tattoo sleeve catches my eye. Hot. Maybe I should get a tattoo.

Callie nudges me. "We could go out there."

"No way," I laugh.

"Come on. This is your fresh start, right?" She takes my empty plate and tosses it in a trash can. "What if you just . . . went for it?"

Maybe it's that cinnamon roll shot coursing through my veins. Maybe I'm high on the excitement of being on Botetourt's campus. Maybe it's the unwavering power of friendship, despite diarrhea-related hardships. Whatever compels me to do it, I shrug off Zuri's jacket and hang it on a chair, then march right up to the DJ station and shout my song request.

The DJ nods. *"Foe missed art in school!"* she shouts back.

"What?" I yell.

"Foam is starting soon!" she repeats.

I have no idea what she's talking about but don't have time to ask: the opening beats of "Tightrope" thrum from the speakers. Callie joins me in the middle of the dance floor, and Zuri and Reena let out a cheer. We always improvise the opening verse, so I lift my arms and wiggle my feet around, channeling Janelle Monáe's confidence and spunk. And then the chorus hits, and Callie and I step into our routine. Tiptoes, squat, tiptoes, squat, wiggle the feet, flap the arms.

> *You gotta tip on the tightrope (tip, tip on it)*
> *T-t-t-tip on the tightrope (tip, tip on it)*

This is literally the only choreographed dance we know (besides our sloppy *Footloose*, which would win us zero style points), and it's a miracle we learned it in the first place. But we might as well whip it out in a party's time of need.

A few women edge onto the dance floor, including Zuri and Reena. Thank goddess.

Then an excited scream erupts.

I turn around, and white, fluffy foam erupts into the air from a machine in the corner. The foam plops onto the dance floor like lava from a science fair volcano. Callie runs toward it, arms in the air. A patch of fluff lands on my shoulder.

I take some in my hand and sniff it—it's clean and wet, like soap bubbles. *Guess my fresh start will be squeaky clean.* I shrug and keep dancing. I protect my face at all costs—this makeup is only coming off my cold, dead body.

The foam quickly accumulates, and we kick it into the air as we continue our routine. Around us, girls throw globs of it at each other, squealing.

Before long, we can't see our feet.

"This must be what it's like to live in a snow globe!" Callie shouts over the music and the roar of the foam machine.

"I was always curious about that!" I say.

By the time the song ends, about half the partygoers have migrated onto the dance floor. They clap in our direction, and Callie and I take a soggy bow.

Reena and Zuri slap us on the backs, and bubbles go flying.

"Now *that's* what I'm talking about," Reena says.

"That was awesome!" Zuri gushes.

I hug Callie, which makes a *squelch* sound. She scoops foam from my dress and spreads it over her chin like a beard.

But before I can even laugh, a flash of black hair catches my eye across the dance floor. *It's Ian.* He's holding a cup and bobbing his head to the next song, watching dancers sway back and forth in the foam.

He didn't mention he would be here. I use a soggy hand to extract my phone from my purse. I'll be there! he wrote in response to my Sheep party invitation.

"Ready to blow this Popsicle stand?" Reena asks.

Sure, I want to go say hi. But what if he's an Ian lookalike? Or what if someone else stole his photos and has been pretending to be him this whole time? What if I've been chatting with a kid from our high school, like Lewis or Ben?

Callie elbows me. "Damn, your mouth is literally hanging wide open, Luce."

I snap back to reality. "Sorry, uh. I just recognize that guy from some Botetourt photos I saw online." My mouth goes dry as I think of the secret I've been keeping from her.

Of course, this is the moment probably-Ian turns toward us, when we must look like soggy, gossiping children.

"I didn't know we were scouting for booty tonight," Callie says.

I roll my eyes. "I'm *not*," I say. Relief rinses down my shoulders. Callie thinks I just saw a hot guy across the dance floor. That's more acceptable than carrying on a secret friendship for weeks. "Plus we can have side quests!" I joke.

"Oooh la," Callie says, waggling her eyebrows.

But before she can goad me into talking to my pretend—okay, maybe *slightly* real—crush, Reena shouts, "Gals! Let's go!" and tugs us away from the crowd. I look back toward Ian, but he's disappeared.

A few minutes later he types, Did I just see you?!

Oh, thank goddess.

> **@lucygoosey:** Yeah! I promise I'm not normally soggy

> **@thesp_ian:** Sorry I missed you. See you at the Sheep party soon?

> **@lucygoosey:** Totally!

CALLIE AND I ARE SHIVERING AND WET, SO
we stop at the dorm for another costume change. Fuck it, I'm wearing the leather dress. And Callie's out of party clothes, but she borrows something from a girl down the hall the same size as her. I put Zuri's leather jacket back on, and it matches perfectly. I ditch my purse, which doesn't match, and slip my wallet into one jacket pocket and my phone into the other. We do another disgusting shot and then head to the *real* party.

I feel light and warm as we walk across campus, my short heels clicking on the concrete. They make me the tallest in our group by at least four inches. But it's okay. Because tonight I'm just another girl on her way to a party. The thought boosts my confidence enough that my heels stop wobbling.

We walk up wooden steps to a white wraparound porch. It's the kind of old-timey building where historical reenactors might show up any minute and teach us to churn butter. But giant flags hang from the second- and third-floor porches, modernizing the scene. A rainbow pride flag, a pink flag with a white sheep that says *BAA*, and . . . *a trans flag*. Excitement bursts in my belly.

Lights flash in the windows, and dance music spills out into the night air. It's something indie—nothing I've heard before. The smell of pot is thick in the air. And even though I've smoked plenty of joints, I'm suddenly paranoid that someone will offer me a hit, and I'll forget how to inhale properly and cough all over everyone.

Not really a first impression I want to make. I'll stick to throat-burning booze tonight.

Callie must sense I'm nervous—she can always tell—because she says, "Hip bump power up?"

"Please." Three familiar bumps calm my nerves.

"It's our first college party!" she shouts. "Get psyched!"

I take a deep breath, and we step up through the heavy wooden doors.

Someone in a gray tank and camo pants appears in the entryway, holding a red Solo cup in each hand. A name tag with pronouns would come in handy right about now. They have tan skin, buzzed black hair, and an elaborate shoulder-and-collarbone tattoo of a hummingbird drinking from a pink lotus flower. I name them Hummingbird in my mind.

"They're with us," Zuri says, pointing to me and Callie.

"Welcome," Hummingbird shouts over the music. They only come up to my shoulder, but I know in an instant they could pummel both of us in a fight. Probably without spilling the drinks in their hands. "Follow me."

We shuffle between bodies into a cramped kitchen, where the music finally dulls a bit.

"Drinks," Hummingbird says, pointing to a countertop littered with liquor bottles, liters of soda, bowls of melting ice, and assorted beer cans. "Sheep parties are safe parties, which means you always pour your own drinks. And measure your booze, if you're drinking." They tap a shot glass against the countertop.

"Thanks," I say.

Hummingbird looks us up and down. "Are y'all a couple?"

Callie drops my hand like it's covered in shit. "No. Just friends," she says in a rush. I swear her cheeks turn red.

"No judgment, just curious," Hummingbird says. "Some folks come here as girlfriends, and they almost always break up. Friends, though, that's great."

Yep, I can see how Botetourt ended up on that list of best LGBTQ+ colleges. The atmosphere feels like a big, gay hug.

Callie stares at Hummingbird as they walk away. "Whoever that is . . . is so cool," she says.

Callie's having fun.

I pour myself a Sprite with a splash of whiskey, though I'm not sure whether that's a socially acceptable combination. Callie mixes all the sodas together in the same cup, which I know for a fact is *not*. Then we wander down a hallway to a common-room-turned-dance-floor. The eighties-era furniture is pushed to one side, and the space is packed with sweaty, shimmying bodies. The outfits run the gamut: jeans and T-shirts, sequined rompers, oversized button-downs without anything underneath, flowy dresses, and even one person in a push-up bra and boxers. My leather dress doesn't look like anything else here, and yet it fits right in.

We pack ourselves into the group and mimic the people dancing around us. The music is atmospheric and moody and dissonant. I feel like a tall strand of kelp billowing in the ocean's currents. Callie ignores the music and does her classic I-don't-know-this-song dance: arms overhead, shaking her hips and shoulders. The most remarkable feat is that neither of us spills our drinks.

Next to us, two bodies press into each other, sucking face as if they're the only ones in the room. No one bats an eye. It's like the gay clubs in San Diego Alex tells me about.

After several songs, I'm drenched in sweat, so I mouth "water" to Callie. She nods, and we both head to the kitchen. I slurp down a cup of water and catch my breath. I'm overwhelmed, but in a good way. My body is buzzing with music and excitement and possibility.

"I'm gonna rest for a bit," I say. And hopefully meet up with Ian. "I'll join back in after a few songs."

"Mmmm." Callie purses her lips to one side, then shrugs her shoulders. "Okay! But come rescue me if you hear the Callie Call."

I roll my eyes. "Please don't squawk like a bird, Cal. We're college kids tonight."

"Fine. I'll call you if I need rescuing. *On the phone,*" she adds. "And you won't leave without me, right?"

I side-eye her. "Of course not. Where am I gonna go?"

"Promise?"

"Yes, I promise." I squeeze her hand.

Callie nods and disappears back to the dance floor. I pour myself another drink: whiskey and Sprite again, even though I didn't really like the first one. When I peek back at the dance floor, Callie is already shimmying face to face with someone. Hummingbird. When she wants to, Callie can scoop up friends like they're crab Rangoons at an all-you-can-eat buffet.

I shoot a couple of texts to @thesp_ian.

> **@lucygoosey:** I'm two drinks in, and there's no sign of this so-called friend I've been messaging

I wander the rest of the house for a bit. There are some bedrooms upstairs and then a shadowy second staircase that I'd only go up if I were hankering for a paranormal encounter. I return to the first floor, where voices and fresh air float in from an open back door.

Outside, about six people sit around a campfire. A few others stand farther away, blowing smoke clouds into the night air. I take a long, deep breath. I've found the introverts' break room.

"Can I sit here?" I ask a guy strumming aimlessly on a guitar. He must be somebody's boyfriend, or maybe a professor's kid like Ian.

He scoots over on his bench to give me more space. "Sure. You here alone?"

For a second, my body tenses, and all Dad's warnings come rushing back to me. I could probably outrun him if I kick off my heels, but he's definitely got me beat in the muscle-mass department. "I'm here with a friend," I blurt.

"Whoa, relax." His smile is nothing but friendly, curling up within a soft, bristly beard. "I just want to make sure you're comfortable. You a prospie?"

My breath comes a bit easier. "Uh, yeah. My friend and I are staying with Zuri and Reena."

"I know those gals." He sighs. "I remember my prospie week-end. Though I was too much of a prude to come to a Sheep party."

"Your prospie weekend where?" I ask. Ian goes to a co-ed college nearby—maybe this guy goes there, too.

"Here," he says matter-of-factly. He focuses on the guitar for a moment and strums a little phrase. "I had a different name then, of course. But now it's Ayden."

Oh. I look at him a little harder, but it's difficult to make out the details of his face in the firelight, besides his light beard. For the briefest second, I breathe a sigh of relief. This school is open-minded enough that they're cool with a trans man enrolling. But on the other hand, does the school let him attend because they don't believe he's really a man?

Then a whole new anxiety tornado starts spiraling in my brain. Can he tell *I'm* trans? I took this trip hoping I could just blend in with all the cis ladies. But part of me is dying to just blurt my whole life story to him. Then at least I'd be able to ask him all my questions.

"I'm Lucy," I say. "Nice to meet you." I shake his hand, which is small in mine. *He can tell, he can tell.* "So what's it like, um, going to a women's school?"

His fingers pick out a scale on the guitar strings. "I love Bote-tourt. I've made friends who've changed my life forever. I wasn't out as a man when I applied, obviously. But coming here, things finally clicked for me. I felt safe and sure enough to live as my true self. And everyone was so, so welcoming."

I nod along. "Wow."

"But it also sucks in some gigantic ways. People will brag about how queer-friendly our campus is and in the same breath tell me I don't belong—'cause they assume I don't go here. And, like, class discussions will veer into TERF territory and the professors won't stop it. It's been happening for years, but the administration has never taken it seriously. We had to fight so hard to even get the graduation policy changed for trans guys and nonbinary folks. But I don't think I would've been brave enough to accept who I am anywhere else."

I want to ask so many questions. Are there trans women here? What's the name and pronoun policy? And what name will they read for Ayden at graduation? I want to tell him how awesome he is, and how happy I am that he's out. "Thanks for telling me your story" is the closest I get. "I'm, uh, in favor." *Stupid, stupid.*

"There's actually a protest tomorrow morning outside the admin building. We figure if we make a fuss in front of prospective students and their parents, the board of trustees can't just ignore us again."

"Wow. Good luck with it." And then I can't get my mouth to say another word. My superpower: being awkwardly silent in any situation.

Ayden fingers the strings for a few more moments. "You need help finding your friend?" he asks. "Not that I mind keeping you company."

"Oh, um, no." I give an awkward laugh. "She's on the dance floor. I just needed a break."

"Ah." He nods toward a back balcony I haven't noticed before, where two bodies press against each other in an extended mouth hug. "It can get a little hot and heavy at these things."

Wavy dirty-blond hair? Black crop top borrowed from the girl down the hall? *Holy fuck, it's Callie.*

And she's making out with Hummingbird.

Jealousy floods through me. I leave her alone for fifteen minutes, and she ends up on her own side quest—a balcony make-out session?

The sum of all my dating experience is making out with Andy Blake at our cast party three years ago when everyone thought I was a gay guy. And I've crushed on random internet people plenty. I'll just scroll through TikTok like, *Wow, this human is so pretty and queer and funny. I would enjoy slurping that face.* But I think I'd need to overthink a potential romance for a minimum of two weeks before making a move. For Callie, it takes more like four minutes.

Also, is Callie queer?

"Anyway," Ayden continues, "what made you want to visit Botetourt?"

I swallow, turning away so the balcony is out of view. I put the Callie query on the back burner for now. "The inclusive community is big for me," I say. "Figured I'd come check it out, see if I fit in."

"And what's your conclusion?"

"So far, I love it. I really feel like I've found a home. I blend in." And it's true. No one has given me a second look sleeping in a women's dorm or using the women's restroom, and no one has used the wrong pronouns. At school, teachers and kids are still messing up—sometimes by accident but often not.

"Hmm." Ayden nods, thinking. "Fitting in doesn't always mean blending in. I stand out more than just about anyone, but I still fit."

I freeze, realizing I may have just outed myself. Why else would I be worried about blending in? But I swallow and smile. Maybe Ayden didn't read into it. "Wow. That's deep," I say.

"You should come to our demonstration tomorrow," Ayden says, turning his attention back to his strumming. "You might meet some folks worth talking to."

I nod. "Okay."

Then a hand lands on my shoulder. "You're hard to find," a low voice behind me says.

I turn. It's Ian.

10

THE REFLECTION OF THE CAMPFIRE

flickers on his face and makes his hair look like it's dancing. "Oh!" My heart gallops out of my chest. I stand up quickly, then feel awkward about it and cross my eyes. *Cheese and rice, what's wrong with me?*

Ian laughs, though. "It's so nice to meet you. I'm Ian."

"Um, I'm Lucy." The booze must convince me that a hair flip is necessary, but my grown-out bangs just end up in my face.

"You changed." He looks me up and down. He's a few inches taller than me, thank goddess.

"Yeah, turns out foam is really cold and wet."

"Well, I love the outfit," he says.

My chest warms like a roll fresh from the oven. "Want to join us?" I ask, gesturing to an empty bench around the fire. Ayden continues strumming, in his own little world.

Ian sits down. "So how was the drive? Must've been a long day," he says.

"It was long, but worth it." I smile.

He smiles back. "Yeah? Do you like it better here so far?"

"Huh?" *Better than what?* Then the story comes rushing back to me: I'm a twenty-year-old transfer student looking to get out of Central. "Ohhh," I laugh. "Sorry." I swirl the drink in my cup. "I've had a few of these. Um, yeah, so far it's way better than Central. Just smaller, more beautiful, and all that. But I haven't even gotten to see the theater yet. And that's kind of why I'm here."

Ian stands up. "Wanna take a look? I pretty much grew up in that building, so I can give the deluxe tour."

I don't even realize his hand is touching mine until he's pulled me up from the bench. His skin is smooth and not sweaty at all. Unlike mine.

Ayden pauses in his strumming for just a moment, and his eyes linger on me. "In the middle of the night?" he asks.

Of course Ayden is nervous for me. He thinks Ian is just some rando, not a friend I've been chatting with for weeks. I almost say, *Don't worry, I have mace,* to jokingly reassure him. But then I remember the hot-pink canister from Dad is on my keychain back in the dorm room. *Whoops.*

"Night is the best time to see some parts of campus," Ian says, smiling. "But only if you want to."

I glance at the balcony. Callie and Hummingbird are gone. Probably inside, getting cozy on a bed somewhere together. "I'd love to," I say. And before I can stop myself, I'm following Ian away from the party. The party I promised Callie I wouldn't leave.

As if she read my mind, a text pops in: I HAVE SOMETHING AMAZING TO TELL YOU!!!!

> **Me:** Awesome!!! I'm taking a break outside. Keep dancing!

Now it's time for *my* side quest. My definitely-not-romantic side quest.

Once we leave the noise of the party, the sounds of crickets, frogs, and birds blanket us.

"So, what made you want to transfer?" he asks.

"The theater department," I say, taking a sip of my drink. "I want to be a director, but Central doesn't really offer a focus in that." That's a lie—they have a directing track—so I hope Ian doesn't fact-check me.

"Wow. Most students here just want to act."

"That's fun, too. But directing is amazing. It's like, you have all this control over the show, but it's totally behind the scenes."

He raises his showpiece eyebrows in surprise. "It's interesting to imagine you bossing people around."

"I can be forceful when I need to be," I say, and the booze makes the words come out suggestively. Oops. "So . . . your mom teaches theater classes. Does that mean you get to do shows here?" I already know he's been in a ton of them because I've stalked Botetourt's theater department so thoroughly.

"Yeah, I've done a few," he says modestly. "The theater program at my school is kind of shit, so I wiggle my way into the musicals here whenever I can. They open up auditions to the community when they need those baritones and basses, you know?"

I wonder if Ayden's ever tried out for a play. "And you grew up on campus, right?"

"Yeah, there's a little village-type thing for professors and their families." He points to our left.

"That's so cool." I imagine how different my life would've been if I'd grown up around historic buildings and world-renowned visiting lecturers. "What was it like?"

"For one thing, I've always been more comfortable hanging around girls. And I like that I can still be involved in shows and stuff, even though I don't go to school here."

"Graduating at the end of this year, right?"

Ian lets out a big sigh. "Yep. And before you ask, I'm not sure what's next."

"I wasn't going to ask." I totally was. "Do you, uh, work or anything?"

"I do have a job, as an artist, actually."

"Wow, really?"

"Yeah, of the sandwich variety."

Oh. He works at Subway. "We need brave sandwich artists to feed the hungry masses. You do noble work."

"You look really good tonight, by the way," he says, out of the blue.

A giggle tumbles out of my mouth. "Um, thanks! I, uh, love your eyebrows." *Who's the serial killer now?* I scold myself.

But he laughs, and it's an effortless, suede laugh that sounds like the opening to a song. "Thanks, I try to keep them nice."

"Do you?"

"No. I have my Italian ancestors to thank for them."

"Oh. And your . . . who are your other ancestors?"

He smiles, and I wish I'd just waited for him to tell me. "Korean."

"You must have the most delicious Thanksgivings."

Another beautiful laugh. "You'd think. If my parents could stand each other. My dad lives in Seattle."

Shit. "Well, I win the prize for worst conversationalist."

"It's cool. Thanksgivings *are* delicious, because we usually do it potluck style at my mom's house with the international students who stay here over break."

"That's awesome." My mind races with a new image of my life at Botetourt: me and Ian and Callie sitting at a dinner table packed with tikka masala and spring rolls and empanadas and pierogies and stuffed grape leaves. I bet I could impress his mom with my family's hash brown casserole recipe.

Soon we reach an ancient, creaky-looking building with wide steps leading up to a row of white columns. The theater. I recognize it from the website, even in the cloudy moonlight.

Ian leads me to a side door, and a key glints in the lamplight as he turns it in the lock. As the door groans open, I inhale the unmistakably theater-y scent of the auditorium. Airy, but slightly dusty, like very old carpet. I'm at home.

With one *crack* of a light switch, the floor lights of the auditorium illuminate. "Just enough for you to take a look," Ian reassures me. "I don't want anyone outside to get curious." Works for me. Dim lighting hides the parts of me I'm not ready for Ian to notice yet.

Hundreds of red-upholstered folding seats stretch out in front of us, facing a grand stage draped in a heavy velvet curtain. Gold-plated leaves and wreaths form a border around it. The space is humongous. And definitely the kind of place that would be haunted by a masked ghost living behind the orchestra pit. Exactly my vibe.

Ian leads me farther into the seating area and points to the ceiling. Hanging above us is an enormous, multitiered crystal chandelier. It's not lit, and the soft light from the floor glints off it with equal parts beauty and creepiness. Also exactly my vibe.

"Damn," I say. "This is the fanciest theater I've ever seen."

"We've got some bougie-ass donors, that's all I can say. It has three thousand crystals. My mom led the restoration after it started falling down when I was a kid."

I take a few steps to the side, should the theater ghost decide tonight is a good time to finish the job.

Next, Ian leads me up to the stage, where we slip behind the heavy velvet curtain. Painted set pieces and antique furniture are arranged artfully on the stage. "These must be for *Party of Possum*," I say. He raises an eyebrow, so I add, "The dress rehearsal is on our schedule."

"Sweet. You'll love it. It's a nineteenth-century murder mystery."

"Are you in it?"

"Nope, but I'm tight with the director, if you'd like a little intro tomorrow night."

Hopefully the light is dim enough that he doesn't see my jaw drop. "Are you kidding me? I'd love that."

Ian winks. "It's a date, then."

My breath catches a little. But if Ian realizes the awkwardness of his wording, he doesn't show it.

Next, he leads me through the wings and up a wooden staircase painted black. He whips out his phone flashlight, and I totter behind him in my heels. Despite how rickety the stairs look, they don't creak. Ian presses through a door that I can't even see and flips a light switch, and a single row of overhead lights flickers on.

We're standing in a cluttered room of costume racks, open wardrobes full of hats and fur coats, mismatched set pieces, and boxes of all sorts of theater flotsam and jetsam. And there in a shadowy corner, like in any good costume-and-prop room, is an old couch. It's faded avocado green with beige tassels hanging from the bottom. The dark red-brown stain on the left back cushion rounds out the vibe.

I sit down—on the nonbloodstained side—and a little cloud of dust puffs up around me. "Every theater worth its salt has an old couch," I say, spreading my arms out along the back of it.

Ian places a feathered top hat gingerly on his head. "And every old couch worth its salt has an immaculately dressed woman resting atop it."

I blush and become extremely interested in the pattern stitched into the couch cushions. He can't seriously be flirting with me. Can he?

"Sorry, I didn't mean to make you uncomfortable," he says with so much kindness, I blush harder.

"You didn't!" I say hurriedly, forcing myself to look at him. My heart explodes like popcorn in a vintage cooker. A boy with *that* face is flirting with *moi*?

I know tons of other high school seniors who've never really been with anyone, but I still have this feeling like I'm running behind schedule. The thing with Andy Blake never evolved beyond a make-out session. And there was a monthlong fling with a girl named Chloe back in seventh grade, before I came out as anything. It ended after I found her making out with Trevor Meadows under the gym bleachers during a pep rally. That hurt, even though I wasn't particularly sad about our relationship ending.

But if I found Ian making out with Trevor Meadows under the bleachers, that might be a different story.

"I've, um, actually been trapped on a remote homestead under my father's control for my entire life," I say in as even a tone as I can manage. "This is the first time I'm meeting a real-life boy." Miranda to the rescue.

Ian snorts. But it's a cute snort.

Okay, so maybe this is a big crush. Not an itty-bitty one.

"Well, I'm honored to be the first," he says. Again with that kind, kind smile. Then he touches my hand, and pixie-stick dust sparkles up my arm.

I let out a nervous laugh, and he lets go.

"Sorry," he says quickly.

"It's okay!" I grab his hand back and put it on my knee. "I'm just a tiny bit self-conscious." Maybe a braver, more confident person would start the "Hey, I'm trans" conversation right now. But I'm sure as Hellmann's mayo not about to bring it up.

He smiles with so much kindness, it hurts. "You? I can't even guess a single thing you'd be self-conscious about. Ms. Badass in a Leather Dress."

Um, just every crevice of my body that testosterone fucked over before I could get hormone blockers or estrogen. No big deal.

Part of me longs to be honest with him, but I'm not ready to tell him I'm trans. I settle for a tiny, true piece of the puzzle. "I compare myself to other women too much. Like, women in movies or models or whatever."

"Those women are all silicone and photo editing. And look around—" He gestures to the room. "No one here to compare yourself to."

"That's not true. I'm sure there's a cute Victorian-era ghost in a nightgown who roams around."

He cracks up again. "Well, you're the prettiest girl *I* can see."

Oh. My. Goddess.

"And I guess that makes you the luckiest guy *I* can see," I joke. That line was definitely the booze. Every inch of my skin hums with nervousness.

He smiles, and then our bodies move toward each other like two meteors trapped in a gravitational force I couldn't break out of if I tried. This play is getting good.

Our lips meet, and it starts as a regular kiss. But then Ian's mouth softens, and his warm tongue slips between my lips. It's very soft, and very wet. But I like it. I'm not quite sure if my tongue is supposed to, like, tangle up with his in *my* mouth, or if I'm supposed to push my tongue into *his* mouth. So I just leave it where it is but make a light gasping noise to let him know I'm into it.

But the curtains don't close to end the scene, and Ian gently pulls my body closer. *Shit, where are my hands?* I place them on either side of his waist. A shiver goes up my spine when I feel his ribs through his shirt. His sexy, tempting ribs.

I pull away, plastering a smile on my face that I hope looks love-dazed instead of nervous. "Um, can we take a breather?" I ask, winded.

"Of course," he says, pulling away but putting my hand in his.

The only thing I want to do in the entire world is lean back into him for another kiss. But our momentum is so strong, I know I need to pump the brakes. I'm not ready to explain what he'll find if he starts removing layers. "Could we, uh, head back to the party, actually? My friend is probably looking for me."

Ian smiles. "Of course," he says. "We wouldn't want to have too much fun in one night." And then he winks. *Winks!*

"Lucky for you, this is only my first night in town," I say in as seductive a voice as I can achieve. I attempt to return his wink, but all I manage is a squinty blink.

AFTER SOME DILLYDALLYING OUTSIDE THE theater, we return to the party to find Callie and Reena standing on the front lawn.

"*There* you are," Callie says. She lunges at me and wraps me in a hug.

"Thank god," Reena gushes. "I thought we were going to have to make a report. I'll tell Zuri." She pounds out a text message on her phone.

Were we really gone that long?

Then Callie blows up. "What the *fuck,* Luce? Why didn't you answer your phone?" She gestures to the phone in my hand, her tone a mixture of worry and anger. Callie doesn't get pissed except when she's performing onstage.

I check my phone screen: twelve unread texts and four missed calls from Callie. *Fuck-osaurus rex.* I didn't feel it buzz.

"It's my fault!" Ian says, giving my shoulder a squeeze. "I took her on a tour."

Callie looks at Ian as if seeing him for the first time. "Who the fuck are you, Officer Eyebrows?" She's drunk. Does she recognize him from the foam party?

Ian holds out his hand. Like a doof. "I'm Ian," he says in a suave-as-strawberry-sauce voice. "I promised Lucy I'd show her the theater."

Callie looks between me and Ian.

"We just went on a quick tour," I assure her, trying to keep the conversation easy breezy. But Callie doesn't crack a smile. "Sorry, I had my phone on vibrate."

Ian, probably sensing that he's coming across as the villain in this scene, gives my hand a parting squeeze. "See you tomorrow?" he murmurs, and it fills my body with lightness.

I squeeze back, nodding.

My heels *click-clack* as Callie, Zuri, Reena, and I walk back to the dorm. The air is chilly, and I'm longing for Zuri's jacket. *Her jacket.* I must have left it somewhere. And of course, my wallet was in the pocket. Ugh. I almost turn around and call for Ian to let me into the theater again. But everyone is already pissed at me. I'll go get it tomorrow. It's a good excuse to get Ian to take me back to the theater.

Halfway across the quad, Callie whips around, blocking my path. "Do you know that guy?"

"Um, yeah. His name is Ian."

"*How* do you know him?"

Fuck fuck fuck. Callie is not in a good state to receive this information. But I can't outright lie to my best friend. At least being drunk makes it easier to tell her the truth. "I met him on Instagram a few weeks ago," I admit. "We've been chatting. As *friends.*"

Callie stands there, stunned. The silence is killing me. "Is *he* why you wanted to come here?"

"No!" I say. "I promise. His mom works in the theater department. He was just helping me decide whether I would like the program."

"Yeah, and I guess you decided you did," Callie says sharply. "Sounds like Hughes is in the rearview mirror for you."

Huh? Now I'm really confused.

"Come on, Lucy. You think I wasn't going to find out?" Callie whips out her phone and taps a few times. She flashes me a blindingly bright screen.

"I can't read that," I say.

Reena shifts uncomfortably from foot to foot. "Come on, girls," she says. "You'll feel better after some sleep."

Callie ignores her. "Well, it's in your email, too." She rips the phone back. "You didn't turn in our revision."

What? "Yes, I did."

"No. You didn't. And now I see why." She gestures in the

general direction that Ian walked. "If you wanted to give up on Hughes, we could've just taken the A without doing all that fucking work. Well, guess what? Now you've fucked up the Dream for both of us. I hope you're happy."

I'm grasping at the walls of this conversation, trying to make sense of it, but Callie is already stomping back to the dorm.

"Hey, it's just the booze," Zuri interrupts soothingly. "Let's go sleep it off."

I pull my phone from my pocket and check my school email.

From: Admin@Clayton.K-12.PA.org

To: LMyers@Clayton.K-12.PA.org; CKatz@Clayton.K-12.PA.org

CC: MWalker@Clayton.K-12.PA.org

Dear Callie and Lucy,

This email is to inform you that the Board of Education did not receive your revised script by the agreed-upon deadline. Due to time constraints and the obligations of our busy school board members, they will not be able to review a late submission.

As discussed, your play will not be allowed to move forward in the Clayton High School Auditorium, and distribution of your flyer will not be permitted. This is for your safety, as there are concerns about unhappy parents raising complaints.

Please know that we support you, and we believe that trans lives matter.

Best,
Principal Calvin Schmidt

"Be yourself. Everyone else is already taken."

What the fudge-covered fuck?

Callie is already across the quad, but I yell at her. "I did turn it in. I swear!" She keeps walking as if she didn't hear me.

My heart pounding, I tap through my various email folders. I sent the revision on Thursday night. I'm sure of it.

But there in my drafts folder is the email, with the script attached.

It never sent.

MY HEAD IS AN EGG SAC READY

to explode, releasing millions of tiny brain spiders all over my body. I want to shove this pillow into my face until I fall back asleep, but the sunlight is slashing through the dorm room windows like a battle-axe.

Callie is tangled up in her sleeping bag, mouth open and snoring softly. I get a shiver of anger and guilt when I look at her. Anger for the things she accused me of last night. And guilt for the things she said that were true.

I can't believe the revision email didn't go through. *What the fuck happened?*

Through bleary eyes, I check my phone.

@thesp_ian: Good morning, beautiful

Some of last night's events are foggy, but the make-out session isn't. Warm lips, wet tongue, electric fingers running down my back. I shiver.

> **@lucygoosey:** Morning 🤠

Why the fuck did I add a cowboy emoji? I shoot off another two texts to distract from how cringe I am.

> **@lucygoosey:** I had a great night

> **@lucygoosey:** Thanks for everything

@thesp_ian: Samesies. And you're welcome

@thesp_ian: I'm heading to work, but I'll see you at the show tonight, yeah?

> **@lucygoosey:** for sure 🤠

Goddess, what's wrong with me?

I should ask him about Zuri's jacket and my wallet, but I don't know how to phrase it without being annoying. Plus he has to work, anyway.

Instead, I read the email from Principal Schmidt again on my phone. Yep. I fucked up. The attachment was too large, probably because I included an image-heavy appendix of anticensorship articles as a fuck-you to School Board Karen.

But Callie thinks I missed the deadline on purpose. No matter how many times I tried to apologize last night, she still wouldn't look at me.

I was too drunk last night to type a response, so I do it this morning.

From: LMyers@Clayton.K-12.PA.org
To: Admin@Clayton.K-12.PA.org
CC: MWalker@Clayton.K-12.PA.org; CKatz@Clayton.K-12.PA.org

Dear Principal Schmidt,

I was super sure I sent the script on Thursday night. I don't know what went wrong, but it didn't go through. Callie and I are on a college visit, so we didn't realize until late last night. Could you please make an exception for us? I'm attaching the file again.

Thanks,
Lucy

After the email appears in my sent folder—sans anticensorship attachment, sadly—I grab my shower stuff and today's outfit as quietly as I can and slip into the hallway. After gulping from the water fountain, I push open the heavy bathroom door. I'm alone, thank goddess. I didn't wash my makeup off last night, and my face is a re-creation of Edvard Munch's *The Scream*. If I could get my four-year degree from this steamy, hot shower, I would.

I slip into the green forest-nymph dress and clasp my new-old cameo necklace around my neck. I kiss it for good luck. Then I spend forty-five minutes in front of the mirror trying to get my makeup just right. When I see Ian again, I might not have the luxury of dim lighting or intoxication to hide my more masculine features. *You have to be perfect,* I say to the mirror. I scrub my eyeliner off three times before it looks close to perfect. A couple of girls come in and out of the bathroom, but I ignore them.

Thank goddess, Callie, Reena, and Zuri are still sleeping when I slip back into the room. I'm not ready to face any of them. Outside, the crisp autumn air feels good. And the buildings look even more beautiful in the morning light. Central has one Gothic-castle-y building that they put on all the brochures, even though most of their architecture is boring and modern. But here, most of the buildings have the same stately, red-brick-and-white-columns look. It's beautiful.

I head to the dining hall and load up a plate with cheesy scrambled eggs and toast, plus a huge mug of super chocolatey, sweet coffee. I notice the waffle bar and my heart pangs, wishing Callie were here.

Instead of texting her, I type out a message for Alex, who might actually understand how I'm feeling. San Diego is three hours behind, and Alex would never rise before eleven a.m. except in the event of nuclear apocalypse. But she can read it when she wakes up.

> **Me:** So . . . I have news. Boy-related news.

I could leave it at that and keep the suspense going. But I'm too impatient.

> **Me:** Let's just say I got a private tour of the theater last night and I'm freaking out!!!

131

I use the alone time to recharge after a long night of exhausting interactions. I nurse my mug and watch students come and go, many of them in pajamas and slippers. I don't see anyone I recognize from last night. They're probably sleeping in, like normal human beings.

I check my phone for the millionth time. No texts from anyone except Mom: Hope you're having a great time, honey!

I grab a couple of muffins and a banana for Callie and stash them in my purse. I'll need a peace offering for when I apologize.

When I press through the dining hall doors, a crowd of about forty students has gathered in front of the admin building next door. They're waving signs. *The protest.* My heartbeat quickens. I scan for Ayden.

A few folks wave pink, blue, and white trans flags. Others hold hand-lettered signs:

TRANS & NONBINARY STUDENTS BELONG
FUCK YOUR BINARY
Y'ALL MEANS ALL
TRANS SEX IS SIN . . . SATIONAL!

At the top of the white stone steps, someone wearing a trans flag cape stands behind a megaphone. He has a thin, brown beard and big, circular glasses. *Ayden.* I almost didn't recognize him without the flickering light of a campfire.

"Four years ago, I was one of these prospective students running around campus, falling in love with it," he says into the mic. "The promise of such an accepting, supportive community was everything to me. Well, I got that and then some. I found a place to be myself. I found friends who supported me through my gender journey and accept me exactly as I am.

"Just a few years ago, I wouldn't have been allowed to walk across the stage on graduation day. Thanks to the efforts of previous classes, the graduation policy was updated."

A cheer rises up in the crowd. I stand on the outskirts of the group, wanting to show support but not look *too* invested.

"But there's another mountain we have to climb as a college," he continues. "We demand admission for nonbinary students and more support for all transgender students on campus. There are prospective students here this weekend who may already be questioning or experimenting with their gender identity and expression."

Experimenting? With new mixed drinks and make-out sessions, sure. But I've kind of got my footing on the gender thing. Thank goddess.

"Trans students shouldn't have to hide parts of themselves on their applications to gain admission. And once they arrive on campus, they need assurances that professors and other students will use their correct pronouns. That antitrans comments will be disciplined as hate speech. That our residence-life officials will prioritize protecting trans well-being in the dorms." More cheers and clapping erupt.

My chest flutters. What kind of antitrans comments has Ayden heard? Has trans well-being *not* been protected in the dorms? I'm gonna need some specifics, bro.

A girl with two long, blond braids comes toward me, and I recognize her as another prospective student. "Do you know what's going on here?" she asks.

"Um, I think they're protesting the way trans students are excluded from campus," I say.

"Well . . ." The girl looks around thoughtfully. "It *is* a women's college, right?"

"Yeah," I say, trying to play it cool with a shrug. *And trans women are women,* I want to yell. "But I don't know the full story. I just got here yesterday." I get the sense she's about to say something transphobic, and all the chocolatey coffee in the world wouldn't put me in the mood to argue with her this morning.

"I feel like I would just leave if I suddenly decided I was a boy," she says. "Why would I want to go to a women's school, you know?"

There it is. I clench my teeth. "You don't just *decide* one day," I counter. *Shut up, shut up.* I'm not about to out myself to this random girl.

"You know what I mean though, right?"

Another student turns around. *Hummingbird.* They've painted their cheeks yellow, white, purple, and black—the colors of the nonbinary flag—and one of the pins on their denim jacket says *They/Them.* "Because their friends are here," Hummingbird says. "And they feel accepted. It's just a few old, white geezers on the board of trustees who don't think nonbinary and trans folks should exist on campus."

Hummingbird doesn't seem to recognize me from last night— there were dozens of people there, and Callie rises closer to the top than I do, I'm sure. The anonymity makes me feel a little safer, so I take a deep breath and get it over with: "What about trans women?" I ask.

Hummingbird pauses, then nods. "They're allowed to come here. Though I don't know of any who ever have."

"That makes sense," Braids says. "If they're women, I mean."

My skin prickles, as if a security guard might appear behind me at any moment and ask me for my womanhood papers. "None ever have?" I say, careful to keep my voice steady.

"Not that I know of," Hummingbird says. "All the trans people I know figure themselves out once they get here. Like, they start reading and talking to people, and gender finally clicks for them. It's pretty rare for someone in high school to already be out and ready to apply to a women's college."

I nod, as if I couldn't fathom anyone fitting that description. As I merge deeper into the crowd, I snap a selfie with the *Y'all Means All* sign and think about sending it to Callie. But I send it to Alex instead.

I did not count on going on an emotional journey this weekend, but here I am, I type.

Questions wriggle into my head: Will Ayden's diploma have his deadname on it? Will they read it over the microphone as he crosses the stage? Would Botetourt really let me in? I think about the girl who got rejected from Smith because she had to check the "Male" box on her FAFSA. How many women have applied, only to have their applications tossed because the admissions department thought they were men?

On the other hand, the students here feel like *my people*. They're loving and supportive and interesting, and they're fighting for trans rights on a Saturday morning.

Defying all laws of physics for this early hour, Alex texts back.

Alex: Girl, I have a LOT of questions

Alex: I want to talk about your sexy escapades but first off, what happened?

Alex: Did somebody get hurt?

Me: Don't think so. It's just a protest about trans acceptance

Alex: RED FLAG

Me: What?? The students are super accepting. There's like 40 people out here. On a Saturday morning

Alex: Why they gotta protest?? Something's fishy there. Somebody got kicked out or beat up or something

Me: The vibes are good. I promise

Me: I met the organizer last night, tho. I'll ask him about it

I leave her on read—sorry, Alex—and snake through the group to where Ayden entered the crowd.

"Ayden!" I shout.

He turns around, and his face lights up. "Lucy! So glad you came!"

"You did great," I say. "I felt like I knew a famous person."

The crowd starts chanting, "Trans lives matter!"

Ayden gives a kind laugh. "I'll be signing autographs all weekend."

I clear my throat. "So I was wondering if you'd be willing to chat about something. Like, in private?" That sounds weird, so I add an explanation in a rush. "I'm trying to talk to as many students as I can to, um, see what the school is really like. You know?"

"I'd love to." He smiles like he really means it. "Could we meet up later today? I'd talk now, but I'm a little busy."

We exchange numbers, and I say I'll text him in a couple of hours to set something up.

I speed walk aimlessly, trying to burn off nervous energy but using it as an excuse to explore campus. I walk past a few dorms, the beautiful four-story library, and a shiny science building—one of the few structures that seem to have been built within the last century.

At the theater, I try to push open the door, but it's locked. As safe as this campus feels, I don't like the idea of my wallet just hanging out in there like an unaccompanied minor.

Might as well just make the cowboy emoji my thing now.

No word from Callie yet. Either she's still wrapped in her sleep cocoon or she's pissed as hell at me. Likely both. I head straight to our morning tour without her. I get a little turned around on my way there, and by the time I arrive at the signpost in front of the student center, an upperclasswoman with a no-nonsense bob and white tennis shoes is already giving a speech about the campus recycling program.

Then I notice Callie in the center of the group. Freshly showered. She even brushed her hair. I give an apologetic smile, and she acknowledges me with a nod.

"Hey, Cal," I say under my breath.

"Hi," she says coldly. Okay, so she's lava-hot pissed.

I don't even bother handing her a peace-offering muffin.

The guide takes us on a similar route to the one I already walked this morning, but she has a lot to say about some architecturally significant doorframes. I'm spending most of my brain space trying to stand close, but not *too* close, to Callie. Yes, I lied to her about talking to Ian online. Yes, I left the party when I promised not to. But I *didn't* purposefully sabotage our Hughes audition. And I'm a grown woman. I should be able to chat with boys and walk a few hundred yards without checking in with her.

Callie and I sit next to each other without talking for the rest of the day's activities. The muffins crumble in my purse, and the banana hops on a train to Mushville. We've had fights before, but they usually just last a class period or two. And it's usually because the answers she copied from my homework turned out to be wrong, or because she had a dream about me insulting Meatball. Three hundred miles from home is not the ideal location to have a falling-out with your best friend.

Right when I need her most, Alex texts again: Hellooooooo. Still waiting for the tea, sis

> **Alex:** I'm working on my home mani. Wish I could practice on you

She sends a picture of her long nails, peach orange and shimmery.

> **Me:** You're a pro. I'll take emerald green next time you're in town

> **Alex:** It's dip powder. Total game changer

I examine my own nails, bare and bitten down. I should've painted them before I left, but I'm still clumsy with the brush. I always goop the polish all over my cuticles.

I text Alex the broad strokes from last night's theater tour, leaving out the fight with Callie. I know she would side with me, and I won't tolerate anyone bad-mouthing my best friend. Even when I'm the one pissed at her.

> **Alex:** Sounds 🔥 🔥 🔥

Alex: Can you see him again?

Me: *long sigh*

Me: I think we're gonna meet up tonight but he hasn't texted me since early this morning

Me: Maybe he died at sea

He's at work, of course. But what kind of monster doesn't check their phone on breaks?

Alex: He's playing the game

Alex: Give him time

Me: Maybe

Alex: Not maybe

Alex: He knows this is your last night in town

Alex: He's not gonna let you get away without another snog fest

Me: Ok so if we do meet up again

Me: What do I do about

Me: You know, things heating up

Alex: Depends

Alex: Do you WANT things to heat up? 😈

I think about it. Would it be nice to just dive straight into my sexual awakening like Pocahontas off a waterfall? Sure. But my life isn't a Disney movie.

Me: I wanna go further

Me: But I'm not ready to come out to him

Alex: Then are you sure you want to go further?

Alex: Cause there's only so much further you can go, queen

I don't answer right away as I chew on her wisdom.

Alex: That was harsh

Alex: Sorry

Me: It's ok

Me: You're right

Me: Maybe I just want to repeat what we did last night

Alex: Then do that!

Alex: Do you feel safe around him?

Me: YES

Me: His vibe is super LGBTQ friendly

Alex: But you don't think he'd be so friendly to you specifically? If you came out to him?

Me: I guess I'm just worried about messing something up

Alex: I get it. You do you, girl

Thank goddess for Alex. I text her a ♥ and hurry to the admissions building for my last appointment of the day.

My admissions counselor, Jen, has an office with creaky hardwood floors, a lofty ceiling, and an ancient wooden desk that looks like it would take eight people to move. She's white and youngish, maybe late twenties, with just a touch of a Southern drawl. "How has your weekend been so far, Lucy?" I savor the way she pronounces my name: *Lew*-cy. I feel like I'm descending a staircase in a hoop skirt while a dozen potential suitors look on.

I tell her about my weekend—sans Sheep party, private theater tour, and friendship-quaking fight—and assure her that I'm having an excellent and comfortable time.

"I did have a question about, um, the protest this morning?" I say tentatively.

She puts on a practiced smile and nods. "We encourage our students to speak on issues important to them," she says diplomatically, eyeing me. *Oh goddess, she can tell.* But her eyes stay on my face. Usually if someone's trying to assess my sex assigned at birth, their eyes examine me up and down, taking in all the parts of my body I'm not as proud of as I want to be. I tuck my chin down to hide my Adam's apple, just in case. "We encourage a multitude of perspectives on campus." *Oh.* She's trying to figure out which side I'm on.

"I was more curious than anything," I say, and she relaxes. "What exactly were they protesting?"

She sighs deeply and straightens the papers in my file. Because I apparently already have a file. "We've been a women's institution for over one hundred and fifty years, and we're committed to that mission. However. Our admissions policies are always changing to keep up with the needs of students today. Several years ago, our board updated the policy to formally allow students who come out as transgender during their time at Botetourt to remain here and receive a degree. But we do not accept applications from transgender or nonbinary students. Because we feel that would be disrespecting their chosen gender."

Chosen gender is offensive, but I keep that tidbit to myself. I chose a label, yes, but I was born with my identity. "When you say transgender students can't apply, you mean . . ." I trail off, hoping she'll finish the thought. But she just looks at me blankly. "Transgender men?" I finish.

She smiles, relieved. "Yes! Transgender men. Because we believe them when they tell us they're men. Why would they want to come to a women's college?" She laughs, and her teeth shine bright white against her stop-sign-red smile.

Life would be so much easier if I could just tell her *I'm* trans and ask her my questions. But I'm not ready to have that conversation with someone who just used the phrase *chosen gender*. Especially someone who's actively taking notes in my admissions file.

"So"—I phrase my question carefully—"transgender women can attend?"

She narrows her eyes just a bit. "Yes," she says. "Why do you ask?"

I clear my throat, my mind racing for an answer. "Oh! I'm just really interested in LGBTQ-plus issues. I've been asking this at all my college interviews, actually."

Jen smiles and nods. "So I take it you're applying to other women's colleges, then?"

Shit. "Um, yes! A few!" *Please don't ask me which ones.* Suddenly, I can't remember the name of a single other women's college in the history of the planet. All that comes to mind is the *Madeline* picture books, but she goes to an old-timey boarding school for Parisian children.

Jen eyes me, as if waiting for me to share more details. When I don't, she straightens up as though I'm a more competitive candidate than she first anticipated. "I think you'll find that our policy is one of the most affirming in the country. As a women's college, all we ask is that applicants persistently demonstrate themselves to be women, regardless of their sex on their birth certificate."

What about nonbinary students? I wonder but don't dare ask. They certainly exist in abundance on campus. Exhibit A: last night's Sheep party.

Instead, I nod, as if confirming that yes, this response is more progressive than what I've heard from other admissions counselors. Jen relaxes a bit. "But can I ask what that means?" I ask. "The thing about demonstrating . . ." I trail off, forgetting exactly what she said.

"A student who is questioning their womanness likely will not be a good fit for Botetourt," Jen says. "And for high school students applying for our programs, we find that it's much more likely for them to still be making up their minds."

I clench my teeth. It took me a long time to "make up my mind" to come out. But I never had to "make up my mind" about who I was. It's not like choosing an ice cream flavor. As soon as I learned the word *transgender,* I knew who I was.

I need a lot more answers, but I'm not going to get them from Jen.

As soon as I step back into the sunlight, I type a message to Ayden: Are you free to chat tonight at dinner? If I'm serious about coming to this school, I need to come out to someone and get some real answers.

He texts back almost immediately.

Ayden: You bet! You free at 6? We can get a booth in the corner. Super private.

Me: See you then. Thanks so much.

I start listing questions for him in my head. *Do you think my application will get accepted? Is it true there has never been a trans woman at Botetourt? If I come here, how likely is it that an armed mob will storm the premises?* Even if he doesn't know the answers, it'll be a relief to come out to someone.

Before I can talk myself out of it, I open my text chain with Callie. Twelve panicky messages from last night stare up at me, unanswered. The conversation before that is from yesterday morning: me reminding her to pack deodorant and Callie responding, Will do-do. Which is her funny way of saying "will do" while also implying a big poop in her future. Yesterday, the words were eerily prophetic.

> **Me:** Cal, I'm really sorry for last night. I want to explain and apologize. I really truly thought I'd submitted the revision

> **Me:** I'm grabbing dinner with a trans student tonight at 6. Can you come too? I've got a bunch of questions and I'm nervous

> **Me:** Also, I want to tell you about the amazing make-out sesh I had. And I want to hear about your night

I can't help smiling when Callie texts back: Sure.

12

I TAKE MY TIME WALKING TO THE
dining hall, breathing in the crisp fall smells. The
sun is setting, and it gives the orange-and-red trees
an old-photograph feel. I crunch some leaves under
my feet and feel nostalgic about Ian, as if we had a
midautumn fling five years ago, instead of just a tipsy
make-out session last night.

He did say *It's a date* about the show tonight, right?

What if I misheard, *What's today's date?* and I left him
hanging?

Or maybe he said, *Tomorrow I have a date with a girl much
hotter and more interesting than you, but you can sit next to us at the
show.* That was definitely it, now that I think about it.

I've been back to the theater twice, and it's been locked both
times. I guess I'll just ask Ian to take me back to the secret room
after the show. All my fingers and toes are crossed that Zuri's jacket
is right where I left it, with my wallet untouched. And that Ian

might be interested in resuming last night's scene right where we left off.

But for now, I push those fluttery feelings down, down, down. I've got an important dinner to get through.

The dining hall stands at the top of a hill, with a twisting cobblestone path leading up to it. I'm a little early, so I shuffle my feet through the leaves and rub my finger over my cameo necklace. I spot a round stone with crisscrossing lines on it, like a waffle. I slip it into my pocket to give to Callie, since my peace-offering muffins got squished.

"You a rock collector?" a voice says.

I jump, and there's Ian. Sitting on a bench. As if he and his sexy eyebrows have been there all afternoon.

"Ian?" I choke out. Even my voice sounds sweaty. "Hi!"

He stands up and flashes an easy smile. "Hey, beautiful."

Ian is *here*. Waiting for *me*. Wearing a tight black V-neck. I blurt out the most creative greeting I can think of. "Howdy, pardner." And before I can hit the abort button, my hand reaches up to tip an invisible hat. *You. Are. An. Idiot.*

"Howdy," he says, tipping his own invisible hat.

My body doesn't know what to do. Walking over and giving him a kiss feels too familiar. But the four-foot buffer zone between us isn't right either. I compromise by inching closer to him and swinging my arms back and forth for no reason. *Say something captivating,* I command my brain. I settle on "I was beginning to think you've just been a handsome ghost this whole time."

He lets out a loud, theatrical laugh. "You might have to touch me, to be sure." He holds out a hand, and I grab it. A quiver runs up my arm, and my mind races to all the places his hand touched last night.

"I got chills, so I think I'm right," I say, and my face goes hot.

Even Ian blushes a little, which is cute as hell. "Well, I hope it's not too awkward when my dinner immediately falls out of my ghost body."

I blink back to reality. *Dinner?* Then I notice the honest-to-goddess picnic basket on the bench. Like, a woven one with flaps on top. He brought a meal.

Ian's face falls. "You're free for dinner, right?"

"Oh, um," I stall. "Well, I kind of had plans to meet some friends." I point to the dining hall. Obviously, I can't explain how important eating with them is. Ayden so he can answer my questions, and Callie so she can stop hating my guts.

Ian's shoulders droop and he frowns. "Shit. I assumed you'd be free before the show. I'm so sorry."

"It's okay! I just didn't know . . ." I trail off. *You should've texted me, sexy ghost man.*

"Are you sure you can't?" he asks, his eyes pleading. "Afterward we could walk over to the show together, and I can introduce you to Bernard. He's the director."

My mind scrambles to find a compromise. What if I go inside for, like, twenty minutes, without eating anything? I can get my questions answered, apologize to Callie, and then . . . what? My go-to excuse is explosive diarrhea, but Callie's not going to fall for that without a gallon of blueberry cider as evidence. And even if she did, she'd just follow me to the bathroom for moral support.

Every inch of my body is trembling in Ian's direction. *If I don't have dinner with Ian, I won't get to meet Bernard,* I tell myself. Which is ridiculous, but it makes me feel better for what I'm about to do.

"Could my friend Callie meet, um, Bernard, too?" I ask.

Ian shrugs. "Sure, why not?"

"Okay. Just let me reschedule with them really quick."

Hey Ayden. I'm so sorry, but something came up. Maybe we could meet for breakfast tomorrow? Again, I'm really really sorry

It's fine. My questions can wait.

Callie isn't gonna buy the "something came up" excuse, so I go for the truth. Callie, I'm so sorry. But my make-out man from last night just appeared with a picnic basket. He promised to introduce us both to the director of the show tonight. I have a really good feeling. Can I meet you at the theater? I promise to spill all the beans.

It's fine, it's fine, it's fine. Callie's already mad at me, so what's another hour or two of fighting? And I can talk to Ayden tomorrow at breakfast, or text with him when I get home.

I can't make out with Ian over text.

Ian leads me to a secluded spot between a row of weeping willow trees and a creek and spreads out a gray blanket. The sun has already set, and a chill settles into my bones, so I wrap my sweater tighter around my chest and tug the skirt of my dress toward my knees. Thank goddess for tights.

I nod along as Ian talks about local hiking trails and fall festivals. But I'm staring too hard at his chiseled jawline in the twilight to really follow along.

"So what's it like growing up on campus at a women's college?" I ask.

He leans back and smiles. "Fucking awesome."

"Really?" I'm starting to worry I look like a hunched-over gargoyle, so I swing my legs to the side and lean on one elbow. It's hard to lounge sexily on a picnic blanket, especially when it's chilly out. *Stop fidgeting.*

"Growing up surrounded by smart women? It was a dream." Ian runs his fingers through his thick, black hair, and a shiver tickles through me as if he's touching *my* hair. "But I guess I've never lived any other way, so maybe I don't know what I'm missing."

"I grew up down the street from a combination KFC-Taco Bell. So"—I shrug and gesture to the trees and mountains surrounding us—"you missed out on that."

Ian laughs, and I can't help but smile. "Sounds very interdisciplinary," he says. And even though I don't really know what that word means, his joke still makes me crack up. "But I loved growing up here," he continues. "I got to meet so many smart people and, like, learn about issues that other people don't learn about until they're older. At least around here."

"Like . . . ?"

"LGBTQ rights were a big one," he says. My body gives a little start, and he definitely notices. "You know, because so many girls here are gay, or at least bisexual. That was just completely normal to see growing up."

"That's awesome," I say, nodding. "We, uh, don't have much of a queer community in the town where I grew up. And I told you about the whole trans-characters-getting-banned-from-the-play thing at my school. Usually theater is my safe place, but sometimes the bigotry creeps in."

He raises his eyebrows. "Bi? No, let me guess. Pan?"

I smile. I'm delighted, actually. Usually, people are so focused on the gender thing, sexual orientation doesn't even come up. "Honestly, I'm still figuring out who I am in that department. I definitely like you, though."

"Coy. I like it," he says, smiling. "Well, bi or pan or straight, it's all fine with me."

My heart is twisting in my chest like a bra tangled in the washing machine. *Maybe, maybe, maybe he'd be cool with me being trans.* "So, you were telling me you did a lot of shows here when you were a kid," I say, changing the subject.

"With my chubby little baby cheeks?" He pinches the sides of his face. "Of course. I started auditioning before I was old enough to read the scripts."

"Let me guess," I say. "Winthrop in *The Music Man?*"

He laughs. "Yes. That's a given."

"Annnd let's see. Randolph in *Bye Bye Birdie?*"

"Damn. You're good. But you're missing my star role."

"Hmm."

He starts humming "Be Our Guest."

"Chip in *Beauty and the Beast!*" I yell.

Laughter bursts out of me, and I let it propel me closer to him. He tucks a strand of hair behind my ear. *Kiss me, kiss me, kiss me,* I scream at him with my eyes.

Instead, he touches my cameo necklace. "This is beautiful," he says, rubbing his finger over the white silhouette.

"Thanks," I say. "Thrift shop."

He tugs the chain ever so gently, and I let him lead my body toward his. I look straight into his eyes as the space between our lips vibrates with potential. *Kiss me, kiss me, kiss me.* At last, like two magnets, our lips snap together, and I let my whole self fall into him. The connection is deep and desperate and crisp and warm. My lips part, and his tongue slips inside. And it's a hundred times more exciting than last night because I'm not drunk, and every molecule of contact between us sends sparks exploding through my entire body. He lays me down on the ground and hovers above me, creating a lunar eclipse situation with the evening moon shining behind him.

When we finally pull apart, he lies next to me and twirls my hair in his fingers. For a full minute, we do nothing but breathe, but it's somehow just as sexy as the make-out session.

Finally, he breaks the quietness. "So how did you fall in love with theater?"

The question tugs me back to planet Earth as I try to think of an answer that omits any hints of my transness. Finally, I say, "In elementary school, my friend Callie and I were really into *Adventure Time*. It's a show about—"

"I love *Adventure Time*," Ian says, nodding.

My heart pounds and I have to catch my breath. "So anyway, we would act out little skits as the characters and make up our own episodes. And we'd force our parents to sit on the living room couch and watch us." What I leave out is how free I felt, putting on dresses and feather boas from Callie's dress-up bin and traipsing across her living room "stage" as Princess Bubblegum. Back then, acting was the only way I knew how to be a girl outside the walls of my imagination.

"And then when my mom got cancer," I add, "Callie and I

revived the show to perform in her hospital room. We were kind of ridiculous, but it really cheered her up."

Ian's eyes soften to convey the socially expected I'm-so-sorry look. But then he adds quietly, "My mom had cancer, too."

I take in a sharp breath. "Really?" As common as cancer is, I've never met anyone my age whose mom has gone through it. "That sucks. What kind?"

"Colon," Ian says. "And your mom?"

"Breast."

We squeeze hands and gaze into each other's eyes. And without saying anything, we understand each other.

"So anyway," I say, looking away to break the tension, "theater makes me feel free and beautiful, and like I'm adding something good to the world."

"You're adding something good to my world," he says with another wink, and my heart erupts into a bouquet of flowers. "So do you know what you want to do for your career?" he asks.

"Can I choose a college first?" I ask playfully. Then in a hurry I add, "I mean, a second college." *You're a transfer student, ya Dum-Dum lollipop.*

"Your decision will be made after you meet Bernard," Ian says. "He's so awesome."

"I can't wait to meet him," I say.

We both smile and take in a deep breath. Then Ian leans in, and before I know it, I'm on my back, and his soft, perfect lips are kissing me. A bird trills. The wind blows through the willow branches. The bouquet of flowers bursts from my heart and straight out of my chest.

Vrrrrrrrb. Vrrrrrrrrb.

My vibrating phone slices through the moment. "Ugh. I'm sorry," I whisper. Callie's contact photo appears on the screen—the one of her holding Meatball in his dinosaur costume. *Not now.* She must be Level Infinity pissed. I decline the call and silence my phone.

"No worries," Ian says. But the interruption has definitely fucked up the vibe, and Ian busies himself with the picnic basket. From inside, he pulls two footlong subs, wrapped in Subway paper. "Spicy Italian or Meatball Marinara?"

I laugh, surprised. Maybe this meal isn't Romance Level 10, but I appreciate a guy who can stretch a dollar. Though my ice-cold hands would've appreciated something a little warmer. "I'll go Spicy Italian." As I unwrap the noisy paper, I add in a pseudo-British accent, "I've heard rumors of your exquisite sandwich art, but it's an honor to finally behold it with my own eyes."

"'Tis an honor to please my lady with the fruits of my labor," Ian says, copying my accent.

Then, thank goddess, we start kissing again, without even taking our first bites. This time, I lean into him confidently. The camera in my imagination zooms out like we're in a romantic photo shoot: a boy and a girl falling in love. She's splayed out on her side with her long, luscious hair artfully cascading over her shoulder.

We pull apart, laugh, then breathlessly come back together.

Now his hand touches my dress, just above my knee. *This is fine.* I channel my focus into tracking his hand and anticipating what it's going to do next. Meanwhile, I don't want him to think I'm an uptight prude, so I sneak my hand up under his shirt.

"Brrr!" he yelps at my touch.

"I don't know how you're so warm, Mr. Space Heater," I tease. "Give me some of that heat." I press my other hand to his back, and he only squirms a little. The tiniest scent of B.O. wafts up from his armpits, and I go woozy from its overpowering sexiness.

After I've warmed up, his hand creeps farther up my thigh. Every muscle in my body tenses. "Ooh, um . . . ," I begin, not sure how to tell him to back off in a seductive way.

"Ooh, sorry!" he says, and he lifts his hand.

"It's okay." I grab the guilty hand and kiss it, smiling.

We kiss some more, and my hand slips under his shirt again, caressing the bumps of his spine one by one. It feels good to be the one controlling how fast we move, so I press his shoulders down and kiss him deeply. A symphony swells in the background. Waves crash onto a rocky shore. Wind whips through my luscious hair as the camera pans away to leave what happens next to the audience's imagination.

But as Ian kisses me back, his eyes start to unfocus. He looks through me, like *I'm* the sexy ghost. He dives into our kiss more deeply, and his *mmmm* noises turn into something more like grunts. He rolls me back onto the blanket and grabs my hip, like his brain doesn't realize he's doing it.

"Um," I say. But this time, he doesn't seem to notice. His hand slides up the left side of my waist and onto my shoulder, inching dangerously close to the neckline of my dress. I press myself up and hold his arm down with my own, trying to regain control.

He groans. "Ooh," he says in his hazy, faraway voice. "You're full of surprises."

Uh-oh. He thinks I'm going dominatrix on him. The more I press down, the more he struggles to overpower me.

The thing is, I *like* this. I want to keep making out, but I also want to keep all my clothes intact. But what do I say? *Line!* I shout to the stage manager in my brain. But he doesn't respond.

Finally, Ian rolls both of us until he's on top of me. With that trancelike look in his face, his fingers rush to the bottom of my dress and try to slip under the hem.

End scene! I sit straight up and wriggle out of his grasp. "I need to stop here," I shout, trying to hide how heavy my breathing is.

Ian's shoulders sink and he frowns. "Shit, I'm so sorry."

Deep breaths. "It's totally fine. I just"—swallow—"don't have a lot of experience." I force a smile and a laugh. Can he hear the drum solo pounding in my chest?

Ian relaxes and smiles. "It's okay." He puts a hand on my knee. "I'm really sorry."

"In the fall, we'll have all the time in the world," he says. "If you want to, you know, keep doing this."

In the fall. Ian might not know what he's doing after he graduates, but I'm part of his maybe-plans. I faint with joy, and his warm smile wraps me up like a blanket.

I manage to eat a single bite of my sandwich before we walk back across campus, and then my heart starts beating out of my chest again. This time because I'm about to meet Bernard, the director at my dream theater.

"Relax." Ian squeezes my hand, which is freezing cold again. "There's nothing to be nervous about. Bernard is going to love you."

There's also a tiny logistical detail to worry about: Callie doesn't know the transfer student backstory, which means she could spill all the beans the moment she opens her mouth.

As we approach the theater steps, I take in the details. The front stairs are beautiful and grand, with warm light spilling out from the open doors as students amble inside. A small cluster of people on the white stone steps catches my eye. It's Zuri and Reena. Sitting on either side of a girl. Whose head is on her knees. Sobbing.

It takes me a moment in the dim light to realize it's Callie.

Zuri's eyes light on me. "There she is!"

It's the second time in twenty-four hours that I've stumbled upon a distressed Callie, with Ian hovering behind me like a shadow. *Did she not see my text? Did she see it but is still pissed?*

"What's wrong?" I ask, grabbing Callie's hand, which is wet from wiping away tears and snot. *Huh.* This response seems overblown for a missed dinner meet-up.

Holy fuck. It must be Mom. She's sick again. She couldn't get a ride to the emergency room. Dad found her passed out on the bathroom floor when he got home from work. She died in his arms. And I was six hours away making out with some boy under a willow tree.

Callie tries to choke out a response, but only sobs come out.

"Her dog," Reena mouths to me.

My body collapses in relief, then fear. Mom's fine, but Meatball isn't.

"He's at the"—Callie forces the words out between sobs—"vet hospital. He's"—a long string of crying here—"really sick." She collapses into me and bawls into my chest.

"I'm so, so sorry, Cal." I squeeze her. Hard.

"This is my worst"—sniff—"nightmare"—sniff—"coming true!" she wails. "And you disappeared. *Again.*"

"We've been looking all over for you," Zuri says softly.

The phone call. Callie has been trying to find me this entire time. Shame wraps around me like a scratchy scarf.

I take a deep breath. "I'm so sorry I wasn't here for you, Cal. It's going to be okay."

"I want to go home," she finally manages.

I nod. Of course she does.

I could ask her to wait until morning. I could tuck her into her sleeping bag with a movie and a bowl of popcorn while I sneak back out for the show. I could meet Bernard. I could talk to the theater students afterward and get a feel for the department. While Callie sleeps, I could spend the evening with Ian. In the morning, maybe I could even catch a quick breakfast with Ayden before the long drive home.

But deep down, I've already made my decision. No matter how pissed we've been at each other all day, she's still my number one person on the planet. And she needs to go home.

"Ian, can you take me up to the costume room really quick?" I ask. "I think I left Zuri's jacket there last night."

"Don't worry about it," Zuri assures me. "I can ask someone to let me in later."

I shake my head. "My wallet's in there." Plus I cannot physically leave this campus without giving Ian a proper goodbye. Who knows when I'll see him again?

13

WE SCOOT AROUND THE SMALL
crowd gathered in the theater lobby for *Party of
Possum,* and Ian leads me up a set of stairs.

I'm too overwhelmed to say much besides "I'm
bummed I have to leave."

"Me too," he says, like he really means it. He reaches
his hand out for me, and I grab it. I savor every millimeter
of skin so I can remember how it feels until September. For
now, I force myself to ignore the ifs: *if* I get into Botetourt, *if*
Ian sticks around.

The costume shop looks different with all the lights on. The
clutter is more messy, less spooky-romantic.

"I thought I left it here," I say, walking to the couch where we
made out last night. But it's nowhere in sight.

"Someone probably moved it." Ian opens a wardrobe and rif-
fles through coats and suits and dresses.

I get on my knees to check under the couch, behind furniture, on the floor. It's nowhere. "Fuck," I say.

After ten minutes of searching, we come up empty-handed. My blood is liquid panic, but I put on my best performance acting cool and collected.

Ian brings me to his side and slides his fingers down my cheek. "It's gonna be okay, Lucy." His voice tickles my eardrums like a feather.

"I really need my wallet," I say. As much as I despise my driver's license, I'm not about to get caught on the drive back without it, especially in the middle of the night.

"Shhh." He runs his fingers through my hair, and my panicked breathing slows down.

I want to kiss him. This might be our last chance for who knows how long. Maybe for forever. He leans in, and I let our lips collide. The single bite we both took from our sandwiches flavors the make-out session with banana peppers and spicy meat.

"Maybe someone will find it after you leave," Ian says seductively, his face a few inches from mine. "Then you'll have to come back to get it."

I muster what I hope is a suggestive smile. Then his hand slips under the neckline of my dress and fingers my bra strap. I suck in a breath, electricity jolting down my spine.

"Ha-hem?" someone fake coughs in the doorway.

I spring away from Ian, relieved and disappointed at the same time. "I was just looking for my jacket," I blurt, patting around a shelf of mismatched kettles, as if it could've been hidden behind one of them.

"We're about to start dress rehearsal," the girl in the doorway says. I recognize her from the student center yesterday—it's Frida, the head of the theater society. *Fuck.* Of course, *now* I get to meet her. "What's up, Ian?" she says with a hint of suspicion in her voice.

"I was just helping Lucy find something," Ian says, suave as a bar of soap. "She's a prospective student. I gave her a tour of the theater yesterday, and she left her jacket somewhere."

Frida raises an eyebrow. "I saw a jacket lying in the grass outside earlier."

And now memories from last night flood back. How we were rushing to get back to the party, but Ian and I got distracted by each other's lips. We made out in the grass, and I must have left my jacket there.

"Wow, I'm an idiot," I say, laughing nervously. "I think I remember where it is."

"Let's go," Ian says, grabbing my hand.

Frida raises the corner of her mouth, like she's skeptical. "I'll come, too," she says.

We follow Frida out of the room and down the stairs, squeezing each other's hands in silent flirtation. But when we arrive at the grassy spot outside where Ian and I apparently got sloppier than I remember, there's no jacket.

"It was, like, nine a.m. when I saw it," Frida says. "Someone might have taken it."

Reena appears from where she's been waiting for us. "Find it?"

I waggle my head. "No. I fucked up."

"Could be at campus safety," Frida says, shrugging.

Reena nods. "Worth a try. I'll text Zuri. She and Callie went

back to the room to pack up y'all's stuff." I do a quick mental catalog of my duffel bag to make sure there's nothing that could out me.
My pills should be safely tucked into my toiletry bag, and there's no
chance of Zuri finding a stuffed bra because I'm wearing the only
one I brought.

The four of us walk across the quad like we're on our way to a
casino heist, with Frida leading the pack in her old-timey suit and
heavy stage makeup. When we get to a squat building with massive
glass doors, Frida ushers us inside. A security officer in a blue uni-
form sits behind glass, twirling a pen through his fingers. I swallow,
reminding myself that I'm just here for the lost and found, not a
police interrogation. *I haven't done anything wrong,* I repeat to myself.

Frida steps up to the glass. "Hey, did anyone turn in a jacket
earlier today? It's hers." She points to me.

The man leans back in his chair with that easy, slow pace that
would feel Southern and wholesome if I wasn't nervous and in a
fucking hurry. "Can you give me a description?" He has a light
Southern drawl that I know shouldn't make me uneasy—because
people can be transphobic no matter how they pronounce their
vowels—but does anyway.

I clear my throat and make triple sure my voice is in the right
register. "It was, um, a black leather jacket?" My voice squeaks out
just a touch too high.

He narrows his eyes at me. "Anything in the pockets?"

I nod. "My wallet."

He eyes me up and down, as if deciding whether I'm worthy
of getting my stuff back. "We thought someone'd be missing that
soon."

My whole body relaxes. *It's here.*

Maybe on a busy day, he would've just handed the jacket and wallet over. But apparently this man has nothing better to do than tug my limbs off one by one like a child tormenting a daddy long-legs. "Can I have the name on the ID?" he asks.

Time stops. The color around me intensifies as my brain tries to take in every useless detail—the TV screen of surveillance foot-age, the stacks of pastel-colored forms on the counter, the Botetourt mug stuffed with cheap pens. *Fuck fuck fuck fuck fuckity fuck with whipped shit on top.*

I lean toward the glass and lower my voice. "Um, could I give a description of the wallet?" How was I stupid enough to come here with a whole fucking entourage? Including the man I've begun fan-tasizing going on European vacations with?

The guard raises an eyebrow. "Yes," he says. "But I'll also need the name on the ID to verify that it's yours."

Bullshit. He doesn't care if it's mine. He just wants a chance to feel like a real police officer. I clear my throat and glance back at Ian. Is he far enough out of earshot that I could whisper my dead-name to this man? But Ian must interpret my glance as a request for help, because he steps up beside me.

"Come on, man," Ian says. "Just give her the stuff. The name is Lucy Myers."

The guard shakes his head. "Sorry. No wallet with that name."

I'm ripped out of my body, and I watch the scene unfold from the rafters. The tall, dark-haired girl who should be me opens her mouth slowly, looking like she just swallowed antifreeze. "The wal-let is plain brown," should-be-me says. "It has, like, four dollars in it. There's a loyalty card to Community Thrift Shop with five punches and a State Farm insurance card.

Instead of smiling, the officer furrows his brow. Color darkens his cheeks and neck. "What. Is the name. On the ID?"

I'm not getting out of this. If only should-be-me knew how to make herself faint on demand. A medical emergency is the only thing that could save me now.

So, still observing from above, I watch myself say my dead-name. Out loud. In front of my romantic interest, brand-new friend, and president of the theater society.

My clearly masculine, no-room-for-androgyny deadname.

And even though I say it so quietly that the officer has to lean one ear toward the glass, the name hovers in the air like the scent of weed after a party. Everyone heard it. And no one is breathing.

The officer gives me a smug smile, fishes the jacket and wallet from a cubby under the desk, and hands it to me around the glass. I thrust the wallet into my purse like it's a screaming alarm clock I can't turn off.

Blood rushing in my ears, I barrel past Ian, Reena, and Frida toward the door.

But Ian steps in front of me. "Wait, what?" he says, incredulous. He repeats my deadname. Loudly.

I stop, immobilized for a moment. "It's my old name," I mutter through gritted teeth. I try to push past him toward the door, but he steps in front of me.

"What do you mean, your old name?" Ian asks, sounding confused and desperate, not quite angry.

"It's nothing," I assure him. I want to give an easy laugh to let everyone know this is no big deal, just a funny misunderstanding. But despite four years of drama classes, I can't keep up the act.

"No, it's not nothing." Ian puts a hand on my shoulder, and I tense. He's been nothing but gentle with me this weekend. But even if he's a secret serial killer, he wouldn't do anything violent in the lobby of the security office. Would he? "Why does your ID have a different name on it?" His tone has gone from blanket soft to dagger sharp.

"I'm saving up to get it changed." I say it so quietly, he leans in to hear. I can't raise my eyes from my boots. There's a scuff on the right toe. I wonder if I can buff that out.

"You're a fucking . . ." He hesitates, as if not even he's sure what word is going to tumble out of his mouth. But then the word he chooses crushes me like a boulder. *". . . dude?"*

Reena and Frida suck in breaths. Meanwhile, I die, decompose, and return to the earth, erasing all traces of my existence.

After two hundred years or a few moments, Ian snaps, "Sorry, I mean *trans.* Pardon me for not being PC, after being lied to for weeks." Then, louder for the benefit of everyone in earshot, "Hey, word of warning. Stay away from this lying asshole."

"What the *fuck?*" Reena explodes. *"You* get away from *her,* creep!"

If my body were more than a muddy, shitty puddle at the moment, I would tell Ian, *I didn't lie. The driver's license is the lie.* But even if I had a mouth, this is a conversation for two people to have in private, with space for questions and processing and kindness. I manage to choke out, "But you liked me."

"Did you seriously think I wasn't going to find out?" Ian shouts.

166

We've left the safety office and are standing at the corner of the front quad. Students turn to look at us. "You were just trying to fuck me by the creek. And you seriously thought I wasn't going to notice?"

Me? Trying to fuck *him?* I have to hold back a wry laugh.

"Ian, I don't give a fuck who your mom is," Frida says, getting right in his face. "You're gonna turn around and get your ass off this campus before I remove it for you."

Ian ignores her, looks at me with fiery eyes. "Annnnd the lying bastard has nothing to say," he says. "Figures." And finally, he turns around and stalks away.

I stare at the hands that couldn't stay off me ten minutes ago. I remember the lips that couldn't wait to kiss me one more time. What changed?

I'm vaguely aware of an arm around my shoulder, a hand squeezing mine. "Lucy, that was not okay," Reena is saying. "Are you all right?"

"What the actual *fuck?*" Frida spits. "And that security guy— are you kidding me? He should lose his job for that."

My mouth is a sand pit, so there's no point trying to respond. I hand Zuri's jacket to Reena and drag my body to the parking lot, where Callie's waiting with our bags. I don't need to think anymore. I just need this body to get me and Callie home.

14

IN EVERY WAY THE DRIVE TO
Botetourt was a rainbow dance party, the drive
home is the graveyard shift at a crematorium. We
don't talk. We don't eat snacks. We don't listen to
music. The only soundtrack is Callie's sobs, occasional
directions from Google Maps, and Ian's words echoing
in my head over and over and over again. *You're a fucking
dude?*

It'd be one thing if he was some conservative college bro in
khaki shorts and a polo. But he's . . . *Ian.*

After an hour or so, a robotic voice with an Australian accent
breaks through the silence. "Message from Stepmama Mia: Vet
thinks it could've been a really big slushie."

"Jesus Christ!" I shout, swerving onto the shoulder.

Callie jolts up, grabbing for her phone. It's connected to Bluetooth, so the messages are blasting through the car speakers at a
ridiculous volume.

"Message from Stepmama Mia: Sorry, seizure," the voice adds. "Message from Stepmama Mia: Goddamn autocorrect."

Callie shoots a text back.

"Message from Stepmama Mia," the Australian car ghost says. "Don't be ridiculous. How would someone poison an indoor dog?"

"Could you, uh, turn that off?" I say.

At the next exit, I pull into a gas station. While I fill up, I can't stop myself from checking Ian's Instagram account. *Sorry, This Page Isn't Available.* Shit sticks. He already blocked me.

I swallow back tears—we need at least one noncrying driver on this trip—and delete the app from my phone. Inside the gas station, I fill up a big Styrofoam cup with stale coffee. Then I grab two hot dogs and two donuts from the case. Callie probably ate even less dinner than the one bite of sandwich I had. I should eat something, too, even though hunger is the furthest thing from my mind.

"Thanks," Callie says when I hand her a hot dog and donut. She takes a bite from each and then falls asleep. I'm dying to talk to someone about what happened, and I think about calling Alex, but I don't want to wake up Callie. It's ten o'clock. *Party of Possum* is over, and Ian is probably partying with the cast and crew off campus. Are they talking about me? Is Ian telling his friends about the trans girl who tricked him? What's Frida telling her castmates?

Fucking dude, he called me.

So much for my fresh start. As we get farther and farther from campus, the possibility of becoming a Botetourt woman seems more distant, too. I was already going to have to fight: to get my name changed, to educate the admissions council about my situation, to convince the board of trustees I deserve to be there. But now, is it even worth it? Everyone will know me as the Trans Girl before I even get a chance to hang the first poster in my dorm room. Which is the whole thing I was trying to avoid by driving to a school three hundred miles away. Honestly, will any school give me a fresh start? Will I ever be part of a community where people aren't all up in my biz, outing me before I'm ready?

I guess if my fresh start is out, I might as well go to Central. But thanks to me being a fucking idiot, we might not be able to get into Hughes, either. Unless we find a way to salvage our banned-from-school show.

When Callie wakes up two hours later, I'm halfway through the coffee. She yawns, stretches, and reaches for the rest of her hot dog. "Thanks again for leaving early for me," she says. "I know you really wanted to see the show."

"I didn't even have to think about it," I say. Okay, I did think about it a little bit. "You're my best friend. And Meatball is my best dog."

Callie nods and focuses on the hot dog for a few moments. "What happened with that boy?" she asks softly. I was a wreck when I came back to the car, and Reena wouldn't stop apologizing. But Callie was in no state to figure out what was going on.

I swallow. "He outed me."

Callie leaps up in her seat. "What? Turn around!" she shouts, suddenly alert. "I'm going to cut his dick off and force it down his throat. The fucking nerve of that asswipe. Are you kidding me, Luce?"

My face heats up, but I really don't want to cry. I need to see the road so we don't add "car crash" to the list of tonight's disasters.

"Do you know where he lives? Can we slip cockroach larvae

through his bedroom window? Can we mail him some cyanide gummy bears?"

I shake my head. "It really hurts," I choke out.

"Oh, Lucy." Callie leans her head on my shoulder and squeezes me. "I'm so sorry. I love you."

Then the tears do start to leak out.

"Pull off," Callie demands.

"But we have to get home," I argue, sniffling.

"Lucy. Pull. Off."

We come to an exit, and the clicking of my turn signal punches through the tense silence. I'm scanning the area for a gas station when I see it. Grandpa's Cheese Barn.

"No way," Callie whispers.

I pull into the parking lot and turn off the car. The store and restaurant are both dark, but a few cows hang out in the pasture near their water troughs. *Were we really here just a day and a half ago?*

Then the tears fall.

"Let it out," Callie soothes, running her fingers through my hair.

Between crying jags, I tell her the story of what happened in the campus safety office. "He called me a *fucking dude.*" I spit the words out like chunks of vomit. "He called me a liar. He said that I tricked him."

"What?" Callie pulls back, outraged.

I shrug. "I feel so stupid."

"You're not stupid," she says, squeezing me.

"He was going to find out at some point."

"But you should've been able to tell him yourself. In your own time."

I imagine Ian's face again. The look of horror, as if I'd transformed from a cute college girl to an algae-covered monster with seventy-five eyeballs. "I wish I would've told you from the beginning," I say, wiping my nose. "You could've pointed out all his red flags."

"Obviously. First of all, *Ian?* What kind of name starts with two vowels? Come on."

I crack a smile. The weight on my chest starts to lighten.

Callie softens her voice. "I should've made myself a safe person for you to talk to."

"You are," I say. "I was just being weird." I pat around in the driver's door pocket for a napkin to blow my nose on when I find something cold and firm.

Callie gasps as I pull it out, as if I've discovered gold. "Cheese!" she shrieks.

Sure enough, there's the sliver of sharp cheddar I bought at ye olde cheese shoppe. We forgot to eat it. I unwrap it, give it a sniff, and take a nibble. "Mmmm," I moan. The flavor is tangy and rich and creamy.

I pass it to Callie, and she takes a bite. "Holy macaroni," she says. "That's the stuff."

We get out of the car to check on the cows, but most of them are sleeping or hiding. So we finish the cheese by the fence, wiggling our limbs to refresh them for the rest of the drive.

"Can we go back to the thing about us being open with each other?" Callie asks, a hint of nervousness in her voice.

"Cal, if you want more cider, you're out of luck," I joke. "We're *not* breaking into a novelty grocery store."

Callie laughs. "Come on, I have something big to tell you."

"Okay," I say. It probably has something to do with her make-out session on the balcony last night. She's gay or bi or polyamorous or something.

"Well, not *big*, I guess," Callie clarifies. "Medium-sized, maybe."

"Whatever size it is, I'm here for you," I say.

She takes another deep breath. Opens her mouth, closes it, opens it again. "Okay, never mind, I'm not ready to say it."

"Holy cheese and rice, Cal. Are you gay?"

Her shoulders sink in what I guess is relief. "Bi," she says quickly. "At least, I think so."

I elbow nudge her. "Is that all? Why were you afraid to tell me?" I'm not surprised, even though the thought never occurred to me before this weekend.

"I was afraid people wouldn't believe me," she says. "Like, maybe they'd think I was trying to steal attention from you, you know, being trans."

A laugh bubbles out of my throat. "Are you kidding? Have as much attention as you can get. I don't want it." Being trans in a small town is like being the wartiest toad in the amphibian house at the zoo. So many people staring *all the time*. "Now do I get to hear about your make-out sesh?" I ask.

The story flows out of Callie faster than cider diarrhea. "Okay, so at first I was just dancing, minding my own business."

"Your seaweed-arms dance?"

"Naturally. So then this drop-dead beautiful human came over and started dancing with me."

"The one with the hummingbird tattoo?"

173

"Right. And before I knew it, we had our arms around each other, and then they led me up to the balcony, and after a while"— she shrugs—"it just happened. And then it happened again. And then again."

My face cracks into a smile. "That's so awesome, Cal. I'm happy for you."

"Oh! And get this. They're from Pittsburgh."

"What? Like, *our* Pittsburgh?"

"Yep. *And* remember that theater where we saw *Rocky Horror*?"

"The Finnegan? I will literally remember it as a pivotal life event for as long as I live."

"They *work* there in the summers."

"Shut the fridge door."

"I know, right? I've been wanting to talk to you about it all fucking day, but we were too pissed at each other."

"That's the coolest thing I've ever heard," I say.

A young cow walks toward us. It's hard to tell in the dark, but she looks like the same shaky-legged calf we saw on Friday.

"Greetings, baby cow," Callie says.

"How's my awkward little friend?" I ask. Her gait isn't quite so wobbly anymore. "You look like you're finding your footing."

"They grow up so fast," Callie says, wiping a fake tear.

I put an arm around Callie's shoulder. "Hey. There's one more thing I have to come clean about, while we're in the sharing spirit."

She heaves a sigh. "Ian got you pregnant?"

"Worse," I say, shaking my head.

"What?"

"I ate that donut I bought for you while you were asleep," I say in the most serious voice I can muster.

There's a beat, and then an explosion of laughter rips from Callie and echoes against Grandpa's Cheese Barn. I can't help laughing, too.

"That's okay," she says. "My digestive tract is still under repair after that cider."

"My emotional well-being is under repair after that cider," I tell her. "But if we survived Mount Buttsuvius, we can survive anything."

ON MONDAY, CALLIE SHOWS UP

to theater class with swollen eyes and her biggest, fluffiest hoodie. As far as I can tell, she's spent the last thirty hours at the veterinary hospital, reading picture books to Meatball and petting the parts of him not covered in tubes and bandages.

"How's he doing, Cal?" I ask, wrapping her in a hug.

Her voice is barely a frog croak. "The same."

It hurts to see my best friend like this. But at least she's too focused on Meatball to remember that I've wadded up both our futures like snotty tissues and thrown them in the garbage.

Which I'm going to unwad and unsnottify. Somehow.

After class ends, I catch Mr. Walker on his way to his office. "Mr. Walker? Did you hear anything?" He called the school board this morning to argue our case, and they promised to give him an answer "shortly." Whatever that means. Will they read the script after all? Make us do more revisions? Force us to incorporate Jesus's birth, death, and resurrection into the plot?

Central might not be the dream school it used to be for me. But at least I haven't publicly outed myself on its front quad, which puts it above Botetourt. It's a good school. And Callie wants to be there. And any place where Callie is pretty much becomes my favorite place.

Mr. Walker shakes his head. "Nothing yet."

"We should still have rehearsal today, yeah?" I chew the inside of my lip. If we don't get to work soon, our show will be a pile of hot, chaotic garbage that probably *deserves* to be banned.

"Go ahead and get to work with the new script," he says with a tired edge to his voice. "When I talked to the woman on the phone this morning, she sounded pretty sure they'd approve it. Knock on wood." He raps his knuckles on the door to the back hallway.

"That's metal," I point out.

He shrugs and knocks on the side of his own head. "Better?"

I smile. "Better." My shoulders relax a little.

As the cast arrives, I pass out stapled copies of the new script: *The Storm: A Retelling of Shakespeare's "The Tempest."* The title looks unfinished without the word *queer*. But at least this packet's a little thinner than the last version—fewer lines to memorize. Turns out the story gets shorter when you take out all the good parts.

After everyone's here, I slide onto the edge of the stage. The lump I know to be Callie doesn't budge. *Guess I'm flying solo into this shit tornado.* I clear my throat. "As you know, we were forced to change our play to be less 'offensive' to certain closed-minded audiences."

"This is such bullshit," Shireen groans, scanning the first page. "Not the script," she clarifies. "The school board."

Emma shakes her head at the cover page, and Martín pretends to rip the whole packet in half.

"We'll get through this," I say with what I hope sounds like confidence. Callie would whip out the perfect motivational line right now. I rack my brain, but all that comes out of my mouth is: "They can censor our play, but they can't censor our spirits." The cast smiles politely.

Miles pages through the script, pressing a pen to his chin. After a while he says, "Honestly, I like the changes you made." He shrugs. "The first one was a little . . . preachy, you know?"

I glance at Callie for backup, but she's unresponsive. *Deep breath.* "You're saying it was preachy because it celebrated trans people?"

He rolls his eyes. "You know that's not what I mean. I'm just saying, this version doesn't alienate anyone."

"Who exactly are you worried about alienating?" I challenge, crossing my arms over my chest to keep my heart from pounding its way out. *White-toast, closed-minded parents who hate joy,* I assume.

Miles raises his hands in surrender. "Don't come at me, okay? Sometimes the gender soapbox gets a little old, that's all."

I clench my fists hard enough to set off an earthquake. *Back me up, Cal!* I scream at her with my mind.

But thank goddess, Emma says, "I don't feel that way," without looking up from her knitting project. "I loved the old version."

"Same," Shireen and Martín echo.

I flash them a grateful smile. But before I can think of a

comeback of my own, the door to the back hallway cracks open. It's Mr. Walker. His lips are pressed together, and he can't seem to look up from the floor.

A brick falls from my throat into my butt. *Fuck.* I retreat to my seat next to Callie and find her hand in the mountain of sweatshirt folds.

"I'll get right to it." Mr. Walker claps his hands together, frowning. "The school board has completely shut down *The Storm.*"

The collective gasp is so loud, I'd swear it was staged. The ever-present clacking of Emma's knitting needles falls silent.

"*What?*" Martín says.

"But why?" Shireen flips through her script. "It's, like, so sanitized."

Mr. Walker makes the mistake of glancing at me, which sends everyone else's eyes in my direction.

I wince. "The new script was barely late," I choke out.

"You turned it in *late?*" Miles tilts his head back and groans as if I've just declined a Broadway acting contract on his behalf.

"It was an accident," I say. "I thought the email went through, but it didn't." *Ugh. I'm a soggy, steaming turd with chunks of corn in it.*

"Hey." Mr. Walker holds his hands out, as if he's ready to defend me from a disgruntled mob. "In my opinion, the board wanted an excuse to shut down the show, and they found one. Their deadline was arbitrary."

Miles mutters something under his breath, but I don't catch the words.

"So, what?" Martín asks. "The show's canceled?"

179

Mr. Walker nods. "I'm really sorry, folks. I know how hard you've been working." His face is so sad, I can't stand to look at him. But I can't look at Shireen, Emma, and Martín, either, because they look like I've just personally punched them in the kidneys.

Miles stands up and throws his script across the room. It lands with a *thud* a dozen rows back. "Fuck this," he says.

My thoughts exactly.

"Please go get that," Mr. Walker tells him. Even as the future of high school theater crumbles around us, Mr. Walker's still a stickler for decorum. "Now, the school board made one allowance," he continues while Miles half-heartedly scans the rows of chairs for his lost trash. "Since this show is for my class, you're allowed to perform it there. Once."

I deflate. *We can perform our show in front of fourteen theater nerds at 2:10 in the afternoon? Stop the presses.* I raise my hand.

"The edited version," Mr. Walker clarifies before I even ask my question. "Not the original."

I shake my head. "I actually wondered if we could still use it as our Hughes audition?"

Mr. Walker thinks for a moment. "We'll need to check whether someone can come during that time. But I don't see why not."

A tiny, marble-sized pocket of relief bursts open inside me. It's *something.*

Miles drops his bent-up script on my lap. "Welp. See ya. If the show's not going up, you can count me out."

Wait, what? "Didn't you hear him?" I say, standing. "It's going on, just during class time."

"Then it's going up without me." Miles grabs his bag and

swings it over his shoulder. "I'm not wasting another day on this shit bucket of a play."

"*Miles,* not okay," Mr. Walker scolds.

"Wait." I walk backward, trying to keep my body between Miles and the door. "You can't just quit. You made a commitment." As much as Miles makes me want to gouge out my own spleen, he *is* playing a lead. Without him, we'd have to start from scratch.

"So did you," he snaps back. "And you ruined it for everyone, remember?"

"That's enough," Mr. Walker says.

Miles pushes past me, muttering, "I should've joined *Othello.*"

As the auditorium door slams shut, I blink back tears.

Without a Prospero, our show is over.

AT HOME, I INCH OPEN THE FRONT DOOR AND

sneak up the stairs to avoid running into Mom or Dad. I change straight into my pajamas and sink into the body pillow in front of my Xbox. Alex is on. Thank goddess.

"Okay, I'm gonna need more details about this Ian character outing you at your dream school," she says. She's only gotten bits and pieces of the story over text so far.

"Hello to you, too, Alex."

"Hi, Lucy. I can't believe he did that shit," she rants. "What a fucking asshole."

I give her the play-by-play with Ian in all its humiliating glory. The parts that I couldn't wait to tell her, about making out in the prop room and by the creek, feel creepy and contaminated now. I was making out with a transphobe. And maybe worse, I really *liked* the transphobe.

"And apparently after I left, he still wouldn't stop outing me to everyone," I say. Reena's been texting me updates since after we left Saturday night. She's pissed and thinks both Ian and the security guard should be banned from campus, but I know better than to get my hopes up. "None of this would've happened if I'd just come out to Ian sooner," I say.

"No. Nuh-uh," Alex snaps. "It's your choice when to disclose. *Yours.* And they took that choice away from you."

I swallow back a wave of embarrassment and hurt. I really don't want to cry again.

Alex continues. "If dating a trans person was such a deal breaker for Ian, he should've been up-front about that. You didn't owe him anything."

The most painful moments from that night jolt through my body. The look of horror on Ian's face when he heard my birth name. The *You're a fucking dude?* echoing across the quad.

"So, what now?" Alex asks, her voice soft again.

I tilt my head back and groan. "I'm accepting proposals for brilliant ideas," I say. "Because I've got nothing."

"It sounded like you loved the school, right? Besides that whole thing with Phobe Face."

I sigh. I did love it. The campus felt safe, beautiful, and unlike anything I've experienced before. And also gay as fuck. But Reena confirmed that the whole school basically knows I'm trans now. Even Professor Chan, Ian's mom, sent me a message saying that the theater department supports trans inclusion on campus. (She didn't explicitly call her son a douchebag, but it was implied.) Still, the whole point of going to Botetourt was to get a fresh start. And the start I'd get there is about as fresh as that sharp cheddar I left in the car all weekend.

But as of this afternoon, Hughes is dead, too. No Miles, no showcase, no audition, no application.

"I guess I'll just do a general app for Central," I say. "There's still a chance I could transfer into the theater school as a sophomore." At least I'd be close to Mom in case anything goes south with her health, and Callie will be able to visit Meatball, if he survives this current health crisis.

"Girl, are you talking about licking lead paint off the wall, or your literal future? You're not even pretending to be excited."

"I'm just still getting used to the idea," I say. "And lead paint is delicious, for the record. That's why so many kids got lead poisoning."

"Then I know of a certain turd slug who must've licked an entire Victorian mansion," she says.

Knock-knock-knock. Someone's at the door.

"Gotta go, Alex." I turn off the headset. "Come in?" I hope Mom or Dad didn't overhear any of that conversation. As far as they know, my weekend at Central went great, until Callie had to come home in the middle of the night for Meatball.

Mom and Dad are both at the door, which is highly suspicious.

"What's wrong?" My stomach drops. That's exactly where they stood years ago when they first told me about Mom's diagnosis.

"Where were you this weekend?" Dad asks without preamble.

Spaghetti and shitballs. This is about *me.* I clear my throat. "At my college visit," I say. Not a lie.

"Where?" he repeats.

I look pleadingly at Mom to add some context. She takes the hint. "Honey, I'm sure it's just a misunderstanding. But I got an email alert that your car owes a toll. In Virginia?"

My heart falls directly out of my butt and onto the floor. *Fuck fuck fuck.* Callie and I were out of cash, so we blew through the last toll on our route, planning to pay online later. But since the car used to be Mom's, the license plate was still connected to her email address.

I clear my throat. "Maybe the camera read someone's plate wrong? That happens sometimes."

"Strange that it's never happened in all our years with that car, until you drive it out of town for the weekend," Dad says sarcastically.

"Give her a chance to explain," Mom says in a light scolding way.

The fact that Mom trusts me to talk my way out of this makes me feel even worse.

Time to give it up.

I take a deep breath. "Okay. We were visiting a school called Botetourt. I knew you wouldn't let us go if I asked. So I didn't ask." I become very interested in the beige fibers of the carpet.

Dad explodes. "You drove two states away? Without anyone knowing where you were going?"

Mom gasps, which is even worse than Dad's response.

I want to explain how at home I felt there. About how, until the Incident, no one questioned my gender or used my deadname. About how amazing the theater is, and how much freedom students have to express themselves. About how, even though it all went to shit, I'd visit the school all over again. But instead I say, "I'm eighteen. I'm an adult."

"And you live under this roof," Dad explodes. *There's* the Prospero energy I remember.

"Let's keep this civil," Mom cautions.

"You can't control me forever." Around me, I stir up a storm of wind and thunder and lightning. It swirls around my parents and drowns out the sounds of their disappointment.

"Until next September I can," Dad seethes. "How did you even pay for a trip like this?"

"I don't know, maybe with the money I earn at my job?" I say, conjuring a hailstorm above his head. "In case you forgot, I'm on my own for gas and clothes and college applications and a life-affirming name change. So."

Mom sucks in a breath and looks at the floor. I regret the words immediately. Going through radiation and surgery and rehab with shitty health insurance wasn't her fault.

"Sorry," I whisper, maybe too quietly for her to hear.

Dad goes full lightning rod. "Oh, so it sounds like you need a little help putting your money into the right places. So you don't waste it."

"What?"

"From now on, your money goes straight into a college fund. No spending money. And absolutely no driving. If you need a ride somewhere, you can ask your mother or me."

"Come *on*, Dad." I plead at Mom with my eyes, but she looks at the floor. "What about my name change?"

His eyebrows lift, as if this reminder softens him. But then, out of nowhere, he says my deadname. Out loud. It drops like a broken tree limb after a storm. "That sounds like a perfectly acceptable name to me," he says. "And guess what—it's free."

I leap up from the bed. "Don't deadname me!" I yell.

Dad's already storming out the door. "Don't lie to us," he says over his shoulder. "And you can forget about applying anywhere out of state. It's Central or community college. Am I clear?"

I clench my teeth. Even though Botetourt isn't a viable option anymore, the demand still hurts.

Mom stands there tight-lipped, not meeting my eye until Dad's footsteps disappear. "He's just worried about you," Mom says.

The door clicks shut. As Mom's footsteps disappear, I sink deep, deep into myself, the way I used to when I needed to escape a world where people only saw me as a boy.

16

SINCE WE'VE CANCELED REHEARSALS indefinitely, I head over to Callie's after school the next day. We lie face-up on her bedroom carpet, staring at the glow-in-the-dark stars on the ceiling.

"This is the worst week of my life," Callie finally says.

The past three days had it all: a public outing, my dream and backup dream being crushed before my eyes, my favorite dog suffering an unexplained medical event and nearly dying. I let out an exhausted sigh. "This is my fault. I never should've looked up that stupid school."

After a few moments, Callie responds, "It's not your fault. Obviously. At least I got a first kiss out of it."

"I blame the school board," I say.

"Yeah. Fuck the school board," she agrees. "And fuck Miles. Our show was too *preachy*?"

"I didn't know you caught any of that."

"I was sad, not dead," Callie says. "Why'd we cast him as Prospero, anyway?"

"You fell in love with his wizard voice," I remind her. "So I decided to ignore his weird vibes."

She elbows me in the side. "You let me cast a transphobe? Come *on,* Luce."

"He does have a good voice," I admit. "He sounded like a movie narrator every time he called me Ham-Bam."

We stare at the ceiling for a while longer. Queen Elizardbeth shifts in her enclosure.

"Wanna go thrifting tomorrow after school?" Callie suggests, the brightness in her voice sounding forced. She's trying to cheer me up.

"I have negative money," I say, sighing. "My assets have been frozen, so to speak."

"What?" Callie sits up on an elbow. "What about your name change?"

I shrug. "My dad doesn't give a shit." And Mom is in dutiful wife mode, apparently. She told me she thinks Dad is wrong but that he's already made up his mind. I let my eyes follow the swooping white texture lines on the ceiling. Callie squeezes my hand. I squeeze hers.

Queen Elizardbeth swishes her strong tail back and forth, and I sit up to stare at her.

"Let's just be like iguanas," I say. "Eat some lettuce. Lie under a heat lamp. Whack people with our tails. Live to be twenty-two."

"I wonder if they cover tail warfare in Stage Combat One or Stage Combat Two."

Asha brings up a pot of steamy mac and cheese. The kind from a box with powder—a rare treat at Callie's house. It's the first thing to go right in what feels like forever.

"So, like, what the fuck do we do now?" Callie asks, scooping the noodles into her bowl. "Hughes is a no-go, unless Miles magically changes his mind tonight, or we find a replacement Prospero. And Bootely-bort will forever be the place where that buttwipe outed you in front of your maybe-future classmates."

"Oh, and my dad has forbidden me to go to school out of state now," I add. I spear noodles onto my fork and slurp them off one by one. "It's Central or community college, according to him."

"But do you even *want* to go to Central?" Callie asks. "Especially if you can't do theater?"

"I've been rethinking it," I say. "We've been hyping up Central for so many years, so of course that tour didn't live up to the mega-utopia I'd been picturing in my head. And it's not like it's for the rest of our lives. Just four years."

Callie turns her laptop screen to me. Our College Dreams Pinterest board appears, filled with images of waffles, dorm-room photo murals, red-and-gold Central sweatshirts, and ads for rainbow shag rugs. The "5 Tips for Hiding a Pet at College" link is new. "Us? Hyping up Central? Never," she says.

Unexpected excitement bubbles up in my belly. So what if the college we choose isn't perfect? At Central, Callie and I would be together, basically having a sleepover every night of our lives. It would be fun. Sure, I'd run into some transphobes. But that can happen at any school, apparently.

Callie stares into space for a while. "Wait. When's the Hughes app due?"

"First week of December," I say. "But for regular admission, we've got until February." Thank goddess.

"So we've got, what, three weeks to apply to Hughes?"

"It doesn't matter," I say with a shrug. "We're down a Prospero, and our show is banned."

"*Pshh.* We can recast him. And our audition doesn't *have* to take place at school, does it?"

I try to think back to the online info session Callie and I sat in on a year ago. One student they interviewed had gotten in with a community theater performance. "No, I guess not."

Callie waggles her eyebrows at me.

"Cal, we can*not* do the showcase at the orthodontist's. There's no stage."

"That would be very creative, but no," Callie says. "What if we can find a different theater that'll let us do the show?"

"With three weeks' notice?" I run through the list of all the theaters I know of. There's the movie theater downtown, and . . . end of list. The one community theater troupe in town usually performs their shows at churches. "How much do you think we'd have to sanitize our script to do the play at Cross Roads?" I ask, trying to keep a straight face. Cross Roads is the megachurch whose youth group plastered the girls' restroom with *No Boys in My Bathroom* signs as part of an antitrans protest.

"Gross, Luce. Don't even say that name here. Impressionable ears are listening." She nods to Queen Elizardbeth.

"I don't know of any more theaters," I say.

Callie's gaze settles on the playbill from *The Rocky Horror Picture Show* last year, when we saw it live at the Finnegan.

"No way, Cal," I say, and tick through all the reasons that won't work. "That's a real theater. They put on real shows. They probably charge, like, a million and one dollars to rent the stage. It's, like, a forty-five-minute drive from here. Oh, and I'm grounded from driving."

Callie laps up the last of her cheese sauce. "Our show *is* a real show," she says. "Plus the Finnegan would love the gender stuff in our play. That's their whole vibe. We could make it even gayer if we wanted. Ariel, Stephanie, and Miranda could have an orgy, and we could give them a whole *keg* of tequila to get plastered on."

"First of all, my parents would immediately become deceased if they watched that." But the wheels in my head are creaking into motion. "Besides, even if the Finnegan liked the show, there's no way they'd have availability within the next three weeks."

"You never know if you don't ask." Callie looks up the website on her phone. "Here's the number. I triple-hot-dog dare you to call."

"No way. I infinity-hot-dog-with-mustard-and-relish dare *you* to call."

Callie and I would both rather lick the costume shop floor than make a phone call.

"Ugh." Callie slumps back in defeat. "What if we call together on speaker phone?"

"And say what? 'Hi, we wrote a play, would you like to see it?'"

"Don't overthink it." Callie presses the numbers, and then her thumb hovers over the green call button. She takes a deep breath and says, "One, two, three, go!"

I hold my breath as it rings. And rings. And rings.

"Hi, you've reached the Finnegan Theater. . . ."

"Dammit!" Callie says, and ends the call.

I lie back on the carpet and stare at the ceiling. "You could leave a message."

"*You* could leave a message," she counters. "Does Mr. Walker know anyone there? I feel like we need an *in*."

"He's never mentioned it."

All of a sudden, Callie whips her head up, her eyes wide. "Avalon!" she shouts.

"What's that?"

"The person I made out with? At the Sheep party?"

"Ohhhh." They've been Hummingbird in my mind this whole time.

"They gave me their number. I could ask them!"

"But they just work there in the summer, right? It's not like they own the place."

"Think about it," Callie says in a rush, impervious to my Debby Downer-ing. "Avalon could suggest it to their boss or whoever. They could tell them how serious we are about theater, and how the school board discriminated against our show. They'll be outraged, right? They'd *have* to let us use the space as, like, a public service to the LGBTQ-plus community."

"Cal, no offense, but this is the most farfetched plan you've ever hatched."

She raises an eyebrow.

I sigh. "But yes, let's try it."

Now that we're aiming for a miracle, there's no point holding back.

THE FINNEGAN IS BARELY WIDER THAN THE
pizza shop next to it, but its Pepto-Bismol-pink stucco and huge,
illuminated marquee make it the street's main attraction. Callie
circles the block three times before working up the courage to par-
allel park. Her dad made us sign a contract stating that we wouldn't
cross state lines in his car, but overall, he and Asha were less riled
up about our weekend road trip. They're probably going easy on
Callie since she's in distress over Meatball, who is still racking up
an enormous bill at the vet hospital.

I tug at the heavy black door, but it doesn't budge. "Do we just
knock?" I ask.

Callie pounds on it. While we wait, we examine the posters
advertising past and upcoming shows. *The Rocky Horror Picture Show*
catches my eye, of course, but there's also one called *Peck* that shows
one woman kissing another on the cheek, and another called *They/
Them/Thescelosaurus* with an image of a green dinosaur wearing a
blond wig and bright pink lipstick. A sense of calm washes over me,
like it does whenever I approach a place that feels extremely gay.

After a few moments, the heavy door creaks open and a fifty-
something man with a shiny bald head appears, smiling widely
from behind a pair of hot-pink, round glasses. "Welcome, youths!
I'm Michael," he says, holding the door open for us. His pink blazer
matches the stucco. "Come in, come in."

We follow him into the small lobby. There's a ticket booth plastered with more playbills and a snack stand with beer taps and a
grease-stained popcorn machine. Last year, the ticket taker drew

two big Xs on our hands to make sure the bartenders didn't serve us alcohol. Which we were fine with, because we'd snuck in a water bottle of vodka to spike our Cokes with.

Inside the theater itself, everything looks the same as it did for *Rocky Horror,* except without the rice, toast, and puddles of water all over the floor. The stage is small, but it feels like a *real* theater, with a velvety red curtain and a balcony. Not an auditorium designed with drug-prevention assemblies in mind.

"You gals got really fucking lucky, pardon my French," Michael says, leading us down the center aisle. "The man who's been doing our Gay Christmas Carol read-along for the last twenty years just died. That's why we have the first weekend in December open."

"That's awful," Callie says.

"I'm so sorry," I echo.

"Don't be. He was ninety-five and a real-life Scrooge." At the foot of the stage, Michael spins to show off the space. "Audience capacity is two fifty, including four wheelchair spaces. Stage is thirty feet by forty feet."

I do the math in my head. Our high school auditorium holds about seven hundred students, so this space is about a third of the size. And I don't have a clue what our stage dimensions are, but they're sure bigger than this.

"It's great," Callie says, nodding.

I smile, making sure I don't look disappointed at the size. It's not like we were expecting a huge crowd anyway. One seat would be fine, as long as the butt of someone from Hughes is sitting in it. "Um, so what would we have to do to, you know, make our show happen here?"

Michael hops onto the edge of the stage, like Mr. Walker does when he's about to start a rowdy class discussion. "I read your script, and that was the first step."

After Avalon made the introduction, Callie and I emailed Michael our original version, the one we wrote before the school board started clucking like transphobic chickens. We also added some more cursing, for good measure. I hold my breath.

Michael claps his hands together. "And I love it. *Love* it!"

Callie and I grin and squeeze hands. A real person who works in a real theater *loves* our show?

"I can see why your dumbass school board banned it," he says. "And honestly, that'll help with your marketing."

"Thanks so much," Callie says. "We, uh, love it, too."

"We can't believe this might work out," I say. "We love this theater."

"I'm pretty fond of it myself." Michael removes his pink glasses and polishes them on his shirt. "So. You girls know Avalon."

"Yeah," Callie says. "They told us you're awesome."

"Flattery will get you everywhere," Michael says, waggling his eyebrows. "So here's the deal. For a show like this, we give you the space for a week of tech rehearsals, then shows on Friday, Saturday, and Sunday. The fee is twelve hundred."

Callie chokes and starts coughing, and I suck in a breath. Twelve hundred dollars might as well be twelve billion.

"But"—he raises a finger in the air—"we still have the deposit from Gay Christmas Carol, so we have a little wiggle room. If you can make that amount up in ticket sales, the fee is taken care of. Nothing due up front."

Callie and I look at each other, nervous. That's a lot of tickets to sell for one weekend of shows.

Michael must notice our hesitation, because he says, "I really, really wish I didn't have to charge young people, but it is literally what keeps the lights on."

A bulb flickers above his head, proving his point.

I do some more math in my head. To earn twelve hundred for the weekend, we'd need to bring in four hundred dollars each on Friday, Saturday, and Sunday. The theater seats two fifty, but how many people can we realistically expect to buy tickets to a show put on by eighteen-year-olds? We can't count on kids from school wandering in after basketball practice. Let's say we charge ten bucks—which seems like a stretch for a high school play, but whatever. We'd need to sell at least forty tickets a night to break even.

"And if we don't earn that back in ticket sales?" I ask. "When would we have to, uh, pay the rest?"

"That'd be due as soon as possible after the Sunday show," he says. His eyes bore into me, like he's trying to suss out whether I'm hiding a wad of cash in my purse. *No, sir, there's nothing but dirty tissues and a pack of melted fruit snacks in there.*

"No problem," Callie says. *She* must have a wad of cash stuffed into her bra.

Michael retreats to his office to let us talk it over. We sit cross-legged at the edge of the stage, knees touching.

"This is our last chance at Hughes," Callie says. "How crazy is it that Old Man Christmas died just in time? It could be a good omen."

"Yeah, an omen that we will literally die if we sign a contract and then can't pay up."

196

"People will come, Luce. We'll make them."

"Or they won't!" I counter. "Then what?" I can't help ticking through all the money woes in my head. College apps are around fifty bucks each, and once I choose a school, a deposit is a few hundred bucks. And one of these days, I need to pay for my goddamn name change.

"I have enough money saved up," Callie says quietly.

"No, Cal." I shake my head. "That's for college."

"And? We're doing this to get into a good school. It's like an application fee."

"It's just so much money. That's, like, a year of waffles at Central."

"Look, I don't *want* to spend it. But getting into Hughes could change, like, our whole life paths, Luce. You know?"

I sigh. "I know." Ever since I started seriously thinking about Central again, the idea has grown on me.

We gaze around the space, taking it in. I picture Callie and me in our costumes, performing on this stage. The seats are full, and people are dressed up fancy and drinking beer and wine. Like it's a real play. The Hughes reviewer is scribbling notes on a clipboard, writing down how amazing we are.

"It would be pretty cool to perform here," I say.

"Are you kidding me?" Callie laughs, leaning back onto the stage with her arms spread out. "It would fucking slap."

A few moments pass, and all we hear is the buzz of lights and whir of a heater.

"So we're gonna do it?" I ask cautiously.

"We're gonna fucking do it," Callie says.

17

CALLIE AND I MEASURE OUT A
"stage" with blue painter's tape in the lobby of
the school auditorium. The board of education said
nothing about rehearsing our uncensored show on
school property. Plus we need to get used to a stage
half the size of the one here.

Deja paces with the script in front of her face, muttering lines to herself. We couldn't bear to invite Miles back
after we landed the Finnegan. And luckily, Deja is a literal goddess who agreed to learn a hundred lines in two and a half weeks.

The outer door slams open, and Miles glides in like a sleazy
game show host entering a studio of cheering fans. "Did you miss
me, ladies and gentlemen?"

"You're out, Miles," Callie says.

Deja glances up at him but quickly returns to her script.

"You've got to be kidding," Miles says, laughing unkindly. "I came to your shitty rehearsals for this shitty play for weeks. You can't kick me out."

"You quit," I explain. Outside, my voice is calm. Inside, I'm cackling like a vengeful hyena.

"Also you're a transphobic douchebag," Callie says, barely looking up from the tape she's straightening. She appears to have emerged from her Meatball-related depression and channeled her sadness into fury, at least for now.

"Expressing my opinion is not transphobic," he says.

"It is if your opinion is transphobic," I say, speaking with more boldness than I've ever dared to show toward Miles. Flying solo during Callie's sadness coma was good practice. "And the part's already been recast."

Miles's eyes dart to Deja, who raises her eyebrows but doesn't look away from the script. "Oh, so you're having a girl play Prospero. How very stupid and creative." He storms toward the door. "You know what? This is discrimination. Call me when the whole thing falls apart opening night."

Watching the door slam behind him feels like taking off a bra at the end of the night. I can breathe again.

"Well, fuck you, too," Deja says calmly. I kick myself for not casting her in the first place. Her voice is strong and sharp, and even in an echoey, tile-floored lobby with a script in her hand, she wields a huge stage presence. Thank goddess Carlos and Andre were willing to tweak her rehearsal schedule so she could do both shows.

"Shall we start from the top?" I suggest in my chipper-director voice, which I no longer have to fake.

We start a full run-through of the play, figuring out new blocking as we go. Every few minutes, the doors to the auditorium swing open as the *Othello* cast and crew come and go. They eye us with curiosity: we are the Banished Show. I like to think they're a little impressed.

By the time we get to act three, scene three, Miranda's world is more palpable to me than reality. Ariel has just spread a feast out for Alonsa, who's hungry and exhausted, and then taken it away.

Alonsa drops to her knees. "What?" she wails, patting around the spot where she's just seen a meal. "I swear there was a table here, laden with food. Are my eyes playing tricks on me?"

Stephanie, her overworked assistant, flips the bird from her hiding place in the corner of the stage.

Alonsa lifts her face and arms to the sky. "Ferdinand, where are you?" she yells mournfully. "I have no food to eat, and my son is gone!"

Ariel steps into Alonsa's field of vision. "Little Ferdie is dead," they say with a mystical flourish.

Alonsa leaps to her feat. "You lie, girl!" she spits.

"First of all, my pronouns are they/them and I'm a magical spirit, not a girl," Ariel says in a mock-scolding tone. "And I can't say I like your attitude." They raise their arms like an orchestra conductor, and Alonsa's arms lift and move in tandem, as if Ariel is controlling them.

I can't stop the huge smile that spreads across my face.

"What's going on?" Alonsa stares in bewilderment at her own arms, which lift, swing, and fall as if Callie is pulling the strings of a puppet.

From her hiding place, Stephanie rolls on her back and cackles. "How's it feel?" she jeers.

"You are being punished for multiple crimes," Ariel soliloquizes. Alonsa tries to protest, but Ariel has cast a spell on her mouth, forcing it closed. "Number one, abusing your personal assistant. Are you aware of the laws governing overtime pay in this jurisdiction?"

Alonsa shakes her head left and right, her eyes wide with fear.

"I thought not," Ariel continues. "And for your second crime, I'm afraid I must rip off a long-unhealed scab. Do you remember a young entrepreneur and inventor, whose company and prototype you stole to make your fortune?"

Another head shake from Alonsa, her brow furrowed this time.

"And to rub lemon juice into a paper cut, so to speak, you further disgraced your so-called best friend by divesting her from the company, essentially banishing her and her young daughter to a remote homestead."

Alonsa turns red like she's going to explode, and Ariel finally releases the spell. Alonsa tumbles forward onto her hands and knees. "You have the wrong person," she says between panting breaths. "My business partner had a *son*."

Ariel throws their arms up in triumph. "So you admit it!" Then, to someone in the distance, "Prospero, she's ready for you."

Prospero—Deja—strides onto the stage, one slow step at a time. Alonsa's face falls. "P-P-Prospero?" she stammers. "It can't be you."

"Hello, Alonsa," Prospero says in a calm yet ominous voice.

"And lights!" I say triumphantly. "Great job, everybody."

Deja raises both arms in the air. "Woo! I'm off book for that scene!"

"Two words down, a hundred to go," Callie says, giving her a double high five.

AFTER WE GET THROUGH THE REST OF THE show, Callie and I touch base with Mr. Walker. "I called in a favor," he says. "And Hughes agreed to send someone to observe your show at the Finnegan on December sixth."

Callie and I start laughing. "Thank you, Jesus," Callie breathes.

"Thank you, *Mr. Walker*," I add.

"I told them there was a hospitalization in the family," Mr. Walker says.

"Which there was," I say, nodding at Callie.

She drops her head. She's taking Meatball's illness with more grace today, but she still gets weepy at the mention of his name.

"Which there was. But"—Mr. Walker holds up a finger—"I'm sure I don't have to remind you that December sixth is the application deadline. There is absolutely no room for error. If this show doesn't happen due to weather, natural disaster, an act of God, mortal injury—"

"—alien abduction of the cast and crew," Callie jumps in, "zombie apocalypse, the Ohio River catching on fire again—"

"You're thinking of the Cuyahoga River," Mr. Walker corrects her.

"—the Ohio River catching on fire for the *first* time—"

"We understand, Mr. Walker," I say solemnly. "No wiggle room. The show will go on, even if we are dead."

He ignores the joke and continues. "Reserve a ticket for your reviewer and leave it for him at will call. His name is Gilbert Gillespie."

"Got it. Gilbert Gillespie. Writing it down." I type the name into my phone so I can stalk him online later. Callie scribbles it onto her hand, and she will sweat it off in about forty-five seconds.

Asha picks us up and drives us straight to Callie's house, saying she made enough dinner for me, too. It's a good excuse to avoid my still-furious parents for another couple of hours.

As we walk through the front door, a familiar furry face greets us.

"Meatball!!!" Callie screams, dropping to the floor. "Oh, baby, I love you, I love you, I love you. I knew you'd pull through. I *knew* it!"

Meatball strains against his plastic cone to lick Callie's face. She puts her nose against his so he can reach her with his tongue. He slobbers all over her, happily.

Besides the cone, a shaved belly, and being a little thinner, he seems like his normal Meatball self.

"Oh, Meatball, never scare me like that again." Callie curls up next to him on the floor, and he nuzzles into her chest. She kisses his belly over and over. I scratch the area where the cone touches his neck, and he kicks his leg happily.

After dinner—pan-fried tofu and garlic kale, which is actually tastier than it sounds—Callie and I take Meatball for a walk, and I steer us toward my house. I have something for her there.

"Do you think we'll pull this off?" she asks while Meatball pees on his third telephone pole. When he's done, she picks him up and carries him. He's not supposed to walk very far yet.

"The show, getting into Hughes, or both?" I ask.

"Everything. The Dream. Being college kids together and then, like, launching our careers or whatever."

"I'm not getting my hopes up that it'll be as easy as all that," I say. "I just want to find a way to be happy. And be myself." If this fall has taught me anything, it's that just existing as a trans person is *way* more complicated than it needs to be.

When we get to my house, I run inside for a present I've been working on. I started it as a Christmas gift but then hurried up and finished it when it looked like Meatball might die. Even though he didn't, Callie could still use it right now. I grab the tiny embroidery hoop from under my bed and quickly wrap it in a plastic grocery bag.

On the porch, Callie unwraps the portrait I embroidered of Meatball. The stitches are a little sloppy because I'm still learning (and impatient as fuck). His fur is golden brown and white, done in long, fluffy stitches. His pink tongue hangs out to one side, and his round, black eyes sit just far apart enough to make him look like the goofball he is. Around the edges, I embroidered pink, purple, teal, and yellow flowers, and at the bottom I spelled *Meatball* in teal thread.

Callie's eyes fill with tears. "This is the most beautiful thing I've ever seen," she says. Her hands shake, a sob chokes out of her throat, and then she's bawling her eyes out. I take Meatball from her arms and set him down. Then she squeezes me close, teary eyes leaking all over my shoulder.

When she loosens her grip, I laugh. "Geez, why are you crying? Meatball's right there." I point to where he's trying—and failing—to crawl under the porch with his cone on.

"Thank you so, so, so much, Lucy," she says, running her finger over the stitching. "How did you learn how to do this?"

"YouTube. Just don't ask how many hours it took." I really should start sleeping more.

Callie bends to show Meatball the embroidery. He sniffs it and opens his mouth to lick it, but Callie lifts it out of his reach. "Aww, he loves it so much he wants to eat it."

Before they leave, Callie gives me another hug. "I really, really want us to go to college together, Luce."

"Me too," I say as we rock back and forth. "Do you think Central allows emotional support dogs?"

Callie gasps. "You think I could get him registered as one?" She gives me one last squeeze, scoops up Meatball, and heads back toward her house. "I'll do some research!"

WHEN I FINALLY GO BACK INSIDE, I'M HUNGRY

again, so I heat up some frozen pizza rolls in the microwave. Mom walks in. "Long day, huh?" she says.

I nod, biting into the dough and sucking out the molten cheesy interior.

She comes up behind me and massages my shoulders, like I do for her when she has a bad pain day.

"Where's Dad?" I ask. We haven't spoken—or really even seen each other—since he deadnamed me on Monday.

"Avoiding you, I think," she says with a slight smile. "He feels bad for what he said."

"He should," I say sharply. And then I soften. "I mean, I feel bad, too. Not for calling him out. But for lying to you about the trip."

Mom squeezes my shoulders. "Thanks, honey."

"I know I should've told you. But I felt bad for even thinking about going so far for school. I was ashamed, I guess."

"What do you mean?" she asks, concern thick in her voice.

"If you get sick again, I mean. I would've been so far away, like Callie was when Meatball went to the hospital."

She hugs me tight. "Don't be ridiculous. There are plenty of reasons to cross a school off your list, but my boobs isn't one of them."

"Or lack thereof," I say with a smile.

Mom laughs, surprised. "Are you studying premed at school?"

I scoff. "Uh, with my biology grades? That's a solid no."

"So no plans to become an expert in oncology?"

I roll my eyes. "No."

"No offense, but I don't need you here."

"But—I *want* to be here. If something goes wrong."

Mom shrugs. "And you will be. Callie came home for Meatball, didn't she?"

"Yeah, I guess." Something releases and softens in my chest.

"You know, your dad might like to hear an apology, too," Mom says.

I hold back a groan. In act four of the play, Miranda calls out Prospero for his—well, now *her*—continued misgendering and deadnaming. As category-five winds threaten to destroy the homestead, Prospero apologizes, and Miranda brings the winds to a quick halt. Maybe it's cheesy as fuck, but that's what I want from Dad. Instead, I'm the one apologizing to *him*.

I find him in the living room. "Dad? Could I talk to you for a minute?"

He looks surprised but turns off the TV. I sit in a chair, and Mom joins him on the couch. It is uncomfortably similar to the night I came out as trans to them.

"So," I say. "I definitely owe you an apology for driving out of state and lying to you. I'm really, really sorry. I want to have a relationship where you know more about what's going on in my life."

Mom smiles. Dad grunts.

"Thanks for your apology," Mom says.

Deep breath. "Also. My name and pronouns are really, really important to me. It's not okay to deadname me and misgender me when I do something wrong. Dad, I would never start calling you 'she' just because I was mad at you." My hands are shaking, so I clamp them down under my thighs. I've never said anything like this to him.

Another grunt.

I swallow. "An apology would feel really good to me, but I realize you might not be ready to give it."

"It was an accident, kid," he says. *No, it wasn't.* "Go easy on your old man."

I pause, using the silence to beg him for a *Sorry.* It doesn't come.

After a couple of beats, I take a breath. "Anyway. In the spirit of being more open, I wanted to tell you that the show Callie and I wrote got banned by the school board." Mom already knows, but I'm not sure how much she's told Dad. "That meant that we wouldn't be able to audition for Hughes unless we found another place to perform." Dad stares at me, blank faced. "Well, we got a great opportunity to perform our show in Pittsburgh."

"Pittsburgh?" Dad blurts, as if the city is hundreds of miles away.

"Yes," I say, keeping my cool. "I'd love for you to be at our show opening night."

I'm not quite asking permission. Because if my dad said no, I would just do it anyway. But at least I'm being open about it.

"I'll text you the address." And with that, I stand and walk up to my room before I can say anything stupid.

18

IT'S THE MONDAY BEFORE OPENING night and our first chance to practice on the Finnegan stage. Of the cast and crew, only three of us have cars (and driving privileges), so we cram as many set pieces into the trunks and under the seats as we can, then shimmy in around them. Callie and I ride with Deja, who thank fucking goddess borrowed her mom's minivan. We sit hip to hip in the middle seat, flipping through our scripts and making notes on the blocking issues we might run into on our new stage.

After we find parking, some of the actors take selfies in front of the Finnegan marquee, holding up peace signs and cheesing for the camera. I was afraid everyone would be pissed at us for dragging this production out, but instead they seem excited to put on a show at a "real" theater. Some *Othello* folks even asked if they could help out. (We would've said yes if they had cars.)

The show grinds into motion in fits and starts. Two sophomores stand behind the light and sound boards, struggling to figure out which knobs control what. To their credit, the opening storm scene does evoke pure chaos, as intended, because the two of them turn on and off every light in the building. And I swear I hear a warthog fart mixed in with the thunder sounds.

When we get to the end of act three, we've already been rehearsing for three and a half hours. A few folks in the crew did a run to Primanti Bros. after act two, and the smell of grilled meat, coleslaw, and French fries fills the theater. But I'm too wired to eat.

"Can we try that transition again?" I say.

The entire cast—including Callie—groans but returns to their places.

This show has to be perfect.

IT'S NEARLY MIDNIGHT WHEN I GET HOME, but my entire body is vibrating like a guitar string. It doesn't help that dinner was a can of Monster Energy plus a single French fry that Callie forced me to eat. So instead of trying to sleep, I stalk Professor Gilbert Gillespie online for the three millionth time. I've already memorized his picture from Central's website so I can spot him on opening night. He's a white guy, fiftyish, with black, round glasses that match his black button-down shirt. He specializes in directing but has also acted in a traveling Shakespeare troupe. Hopefully he's not a Shakespeare purist. At least his Twitter profile suggests that he supports LGBTQ+ rights.

I look through his offerings in Central's course catalog—Intro to Directing; Approaches to Staging; Production Management. All of them sound important and interesting. But I can't help wishing for some of the more unique options at Botetourt: Diverse Representation on Stage and Screen; Theater of Social Change; Stage Combat.

I clear that wish out of my mind, like a snowplow pushing away a pile of muddy slush. Botetourt is a scorch mark on the map of my life. There's no going back.

We have to get into Hughes. *Have to, have to, have to, have to.*

Callie must read my mind, because a text pings in.

> **Callie:** We can do this

> **Callie:** I have a good feeling

> **Me:** *nervous breathing*

> **Callie:** You did great today

> **Callie:** You're getting bossier in a good way

> **Me:** Thanks. I learned it from you

> **Callie:** D'awww

Neither of us texts for a minute or so, but just having my phone on my chest makes me feel like Callie's here. Goddess, I need a cat.

I'm already drifting to sleep when her last text pings in.

Callie: Love you, Luce

Me: Love you, Cal. Always

I'M REDOING MY MASCARA FOR THE THIRD
time. My hand is so shaky I can't hold the wand straight. I take
some deep breaths to calm down and let my eyes linger on the flyer
hanging on the mirror. It reads: *THE STORM: A Queer Retelling
of Shakespeare's "The Tempest."* It's a lot like the one Callie and I
made, but better in every way because Avalon designed it. And they
actually know how to use Photoshop. Last week, the cast and crew
stood on the sidewalk outside the cafeteria—which is technically
off school grounds—and passed out these puppies to every student
we could catch. We plastered the leftovers all over the neighborhood surrounding the theater.

I scrutinize my blue-and-beige prairie dress in the mirror. The
square neckline makes my torso look boxier than it already is, but
I like the way the skirt cascades from my waist to my ankles like a
cotton waterfall. Our costume designer, a fashionable junior named
Cheval, swears it's the perfect "rural homeschooler" look. I readjust
my gold headband, tugging at my hair and urging it to grow longer.
A real homesteader would have long, flowing hair, I tell mirror me.
Then I stop looking at my reflection, because I can't afford a dysphoria attack before the show.

Callie barrels into the dressing room, her bright red wig
already askew. (She thinks Ariel having mermaid hair is the funni-
est joke in the world. Which it is.) "I peeked," she says, breathless.

"What the audience lacks in numbers, it makes up for in support and enthusiasm."

The theater's empty, she means. "Did you see our parents?" I ask.

She nods. "Yep."

"Mr. Walker?"

Another nod.

"Professor Gillespie?"

"I don't know what he looks like," Callie says, "but there were a few randos who looked kind of fancy-pantsy."

Do I have time to go check?

"Five minutes until places," our stage manager, Zak, yells through the dressing room door.

"Thank you, five," we call back.

Well, axe that idea.

"Why am I nervous?" I ask. "I'm never this nervous before a show."

Callie gives my shoulders a quick rub, and my breathing slows down. "Because nerves help you focus and make sure you kick ass out there."

I close my eyes and take a deep breath, visualizing myself stepping onto the stage. *What if I trip on my dress? What if the wrong sound cue goes off, and it makes me forget my lines? What if there's a troll in the audience who's only here to heckle me? What if the theater is empty and we owe a thousand bucks at the end of the weekend?*

"In," Callie says softly, taking an exaggerated deep breath, "and out."

I match my breathing to hers, just to mollify her, but the long breath does calm me down a bit.

"And if you choke up," Callie adds, "just remember two words to make you feel better."

"What words?"

She puts a hand to my ear and whispers, "Mount Buttsuvius." I bend over in a silent, choking laugh. Callie slaps me on the back. "Don't die now!" she implores with mock severity. "Meatball's your understudy, and the pressure would be too much on him right now."

The laughter fills me like bubbles, and my body feels light again. I can do this. "Hip bump power up?" I suggest.

"I thought you'd never ask."

We slam our hips together like our lives depend on it.

AS THE CURTAINS OPEN ON STEPHANIE,

Ferdinand, and Alonsa driving their car through the tumultuous storm, a similar squall roils in my belly. *Did Professor Gillespie get a good seat? Will he get the joke about Callie's wig, or will he think it's childish? What if Dad says something shitty and Professor Gillespie overhears it?*

"Eyes on the road, Stephanie!" Alonsa screams, bracing herself against an imaginary dashboard.

"I'm trying, boss!" she screeches in response. "I can't see a thing!"

"I'm gonna be sick," Ferdinand moans from the back seat.

Alonsa mutters to herself, "Why your cousin insisted on getting married in rural Pennsylvania I'll never know."

Ferdinand lifts his head from his knees. "It was a beautiful wedding, though, wasn't it? Claribel's vows were so touching."

In the wings, I give Deja's hand a squeeze, and she smiles at me. "Break a leg!" I mouth.

She nods and steps onto the stage with her arms raised. "Thunder! Wind! Lightning!" she shouts. "Rain down on my enemies!" The storm sounds fill up the theater, and a buzz runs down my spine and through my limbs like electricity. "Pretty impressive, don't you think, Randolph?"

Here we go.

As I step onto the stage for my first line, the tremble in my limbs hits a 7.0 on the Richter scale. But my first line explodes through the auditorium: "For the millionth time, Mother, my name is *Miranda.*"

BOOM. Thunder crashes through the speakers, and the stage lights flash to simulate lightning.

I know I shouldn't, but I scan the audience for Professor Gillespie. All I can make out is a sea of darkened seats, dotted with a few bodies here and there. He could be any of them.

Deja takes on the sweet tone of a smiling, overbearing mother. "Son, you've never even *met* a girl. You couldn't possibly know what it means to *be* one." She plays the role so differently than Miles did—he was all thunder, and she's gentle, toxic mist.

"You're not listening to me!" I yell. My nerves melt away like butter. Miranda takes over my body, and the performance clicks into place.

215

WHEN WE COME TO THE FINAL SCENE OF THE
show, I'm floating several inches off the ground. *I wish I could stay right here forever,* I think.

Ferdinand grasps my hands and lowers himself to one knee. "Marry me, Miranda," he implores.

"*Marry* you?" I back away in shock. "But you're the first boy I've ever met!" One of my favorite changes we made to Shakespeare's original is that Miranda falls in love with Ferdinand but refuses his marriage proposal.

Ferdinand crumples. "I thought you loved me, Miranda."

"I do," I assure him. "But I've spent my entire life trapped by my mother on this homestead. I don't want to spend the rest of it trapped in a marriage. I want to *live.*"

Prospero appears from the wings and bangs her staff on the ground. "Listen to reason, Randolph. How many men do you think will accept you given your . . . condition." She looks me up and down.

I storm toward her. "I *refuse* to feel shame about myself just because you do, Mother," I roar. "I'm proud of who I am."

As thunder cracks through the theater, goose bumps prickle on my arms. *Did I really write these words before any of the drama with Ian happened?* Goddess, if only I'd read my own script.

Lightning flashes, and Prospero looks around in bewilderment. "I didn't summon this weather," she says, confused.

I step into a spotlight and take a deep breath. "*I've* been creating the storms, Mother. Every deadname, every wrong pronoun, and every attempt to control me has built up like a hurricane inside me."

Prospero sputters, waving a hand dismissively. "Don't be ridiculous. I haven't taught you any magic."

Ariel steps toward me in awe, strands of the red wig falling into their face. "Then—then was it you, Miranda? Are you the one who freed me from the gender binary?"

Prospero separates the two of us with her staff and raises it as if she might strike Ariel. "*I* broke the spell. You owe me your life, servant."

I pull Ariel toward me before Prospero can touch them. "Oh, Ariel, my best friend. It wasn't me." As if we're ballroom dancing, I spin them out and then back into me, then lower them into a dip. "It was *you*."

"What?" Ariel says, their head hanging so low that their red hair brushes the ground. "How?"

I pull Ariel back up and give them another spin. "By not giving a fuck what people think," I say. Though the small audience has gasped and clapped throughout the show, they howl at this line. I hold back a smile. "And by being you, you've shown me how to be *me*." I release Ariel and step downstage. "Mother, I'm leaving," I say, my voice calm but firm.

Prospero bangs her staff on the ground as if she's trying to part the Red Sea. "I forbid it!" she bellows.

I clench my fists and stomp my foot, and an earth-rumbling bolt of lightning cracks through the sky. It's so powerful, my breath catches for a moment. I used to worry this moment would come across as cheesy, but tonight it leaves the air sparkling with electricity. "The harder you try to confine me, the more storms build up inside me," I shout over the noise.

Prospero takes a step back, her eyes wide in fear. "Stop, my love. Please. You'll—you'll destroy our home and everything we've built!"

I raise my hands, and the sounds of wind and rain grow louder. Prospero crouches, protecting her head from the rain and hail, and Ariel, Ferdinand, and Stephanie cower behind a boulder.

"Please stop, Miranda!" Prospero finally says in a gasp.

At the sound of my real name, I lower my arms.

"I—I'm sorry," Prospero stammers, "my daughter."

The winds start to calm. The pounding rain lightens into a pitter-patter. Soon, the stage goes silent.

"I love you, Miranda," Prospero says in a voice just above a whisper. "I'm sorry."

Panting and exhausted, I finally let my body relax. "I love you, too, Mother."

Prospero and I hold each other in a long embrace, and someone in the audience says, "Awwww."

"So you'll stay?" Prospero asks, her face brightening.

I chew on my words before I say them. "No." I pull away, gently.

Prospero gasps. "But . . . why?"

"It's time for me to make my own way," I say. Prospero turns upstage, getting emotional, but she doesn't lash out.

Ariel, who has emerged from behind the boulder, links their arm in mine. "I'm coming, too."

Ferdinand takes my free hand. "And me," he says, "if I may."

"Of course, my love." I bring his hand to my mouth and kiss it. "As long as you shut up about marriage."

He grins and leaps at me with a hug. "Anything for the most amazing woman alive."

Stephanie, still drunk on tequila shots, stumbles across the stage to join Ariel. "Yeah, and I quit, too," she slurs.

Ariel elbows her and whispers, "Your boss isn't here, but I love that for you."

Birds begin to sing, and the stage lights brighten to simulate the sun coming out.

"Starting today, my storms are over," I say, smiling into the light with my friends on either side of me. "Time for the rainbow."

AFTER CURTAIN CALL, CALLIE AND I HUG EACH

other backstage, rocking forward and backward. "I'm fucking exhausted," I laugh into her shoulder.

"Because you were amazing!" Callie says, jiggling my shoulders.

Deja slams into us, arms spread wide. "Ahhhh, that was awesome!" she gushes. "I can't believe I remembered all those lines."

"You fucking rocked it," Callie says, giving her a two-handed high five.

Out in the lobby, I can't flatten my smile as I line up with the rest of the actors shaking people's hands. Even though there aren't many hands to shake.

We fucking did it.

"Got any secret cousins you can force to buy tickets tomorrow?" I ask Callie.

"Yeah, but they'd burn the place down as soon as they heard the word *pronoun*," she says with a laugh.

"Would we still have to pay back the deposit?"

"I'll check the contract."

Mr. Walker swoops in first, presenting Callie and me each with a bouquet of red roses. "I am blown away, girls," he says. "Fantastic job."

"Thanks for everything, Mr. Walker," I say. I press the flowers to my nose and inhale their sweet scent. No matter where we end up next year, I'm going to miss my favorite teacher.

Next, Asha ushers us to the spot on the wall where the *Storm* poster hangs in its black frame. Every time I see it there—next to the one for *Rocky Horror,* no less—I pee my pants a little.

"Let me get a picture, girls," Asha says. "You two are such stars, oh my *god*. Remember us regular folks when you make it big."

Callie and I position ourselves on either side of the poster. Callie holds her roses to look like they're sprouting from her butt, and I stick out my tongue and cross my eyes. I'm too happy for a posed smile tonight.

"Oh, honey, it was so good!" Mom says, scooping me into a giant hug.

Dad hovers a few feet away. We haven't talked much since our pseudo heart-to-heart, let alone hugged. But he breaks into a grin, wraps his arms around me, and squeezes like hasn't seen me in months.

"Help," I eke out, smiling as he constricts my lungs.

"That was a really great show, Lucy," he says.

The *Lucy* sends a shiver across my shoulders, and I smile wider. "Thanks, Dad."

"It made me think." He moves his lips around like he's chewing on the words he wants to say next. "And I do owe you an apology.

I'm sorry for using your deadname the way I did. I wish I could go back and undo it."

Tears well up in my eyes, which is totally embarrassing. I'm afraid I'll start full-on crying if I open my mouth, so I just nod and hug him again. Tight. It's been a while since I smelled his special Dad scent—a little like the woods, a little like sweet onions. "Thanks, Dad. I love you."

"Love you, too, Lucy."

Good thing this mascara's waterproof.

As Mom wonders aloud whether tequila existed in Shakespeare's day and Nikhil runs around wearing Callie's Ariel wig, I scan the lobby for Professor Gillespie. There's an oldish man in a button-down shirt picking up his coat from the coat check. That could be him, if he's gotten new glasses. Or maybe he scurried out of here right after curtain call, in case we tried to bombard him.

Callie and I change back into our street clothes without bothering to wash off our stage makeup, and we hang our costumes back up for tomorrow's show. I take a deep breath. Now that we've gotten our audition out of the way, we can relax and enjoy the last two performances. Whether we impressed Gillespie or not, Hughes is out of our hands now.

"Ice cream?" Callie suggests. There's a place we love down the street that does wild flavors, like fig and honey, Lucky Charms, and lavender.

"Sure," I say, taking the last of the bobby pins from Callie's hair and running a brush through it.

Knock-knock. "Hey, are Lucy or Callie in here?" It's Zak.

"Come on in," I say.

He walks in backward, eyes on the ground.

"We're fully clothed," I say.

He turns around but doesn't lift his eyes. You never know when a bra strap might slip out, I guess. "This was left at will call." He holds out a small beige envelope.

Prof. Gilbert Gillespie is written in neat black Sharpie across the front.

What?

Callie laughs and takes the envelope. "He didn't pick up his ticket? What'd he do, sneak in?"

I wish I could stay in this moment just a little longer—the one right before it hits both of us that Professor Gillespie didn't show up tonight.

But then Callie's face falls, and we stare at each other, wide-eyed.

I check my phone, but I don't have any missed calls. "Check yours," I manage to say to Callie, my voice wavering. My phone is so old that it sometimes doesn't get a signal through brick walls.

Callie digs through her backpack, loose papers and napkins flying.

"One new voicemail," she says, and plays the message on speaker. A woman's voice crackles from the phone.

"Hello there, I'm trying to reach Ms. Caroline Katz." Callie hates her full name. I almost chastise the lady for using it. "This is Gina from the Hughes program here at Central University. Professor Gillespie was scheduled to observe your show tonight, but unfortunately he's facing a last-minute family emergency and won't be able to make it. I'm so sorry. I'm guessing this is a second audition, since our application deadline is today, in which case we'll be happy to consider your first audition—" Callie ends the message.

I sink to the floor and press my forehead to my knees. Thunder booms overhead, and waves crash through the dressing room door. I sink into the floodwaters, willing myself to drown.

My dreams of a fresh start were already shot. Now the theater dream is dead, too. And so we're left to pick up the pieces of our lives. But I don't even know what they're supposed to look like at this point.

19

SATURDAY MORNING, MY EYES open like sandpaper. Why even get up? Every single moment of this school year has been completely pointless. Callie and I wrote a play, directed it, starred in it, revised it, unrevised it, put our wallets on the line—for fucking nothing. We took a road trip that ended in public humiliation, long-term financial restriction, and the near death of a beloved Chihuahua.

I close my eyes and force my body back to sleep.

When I wake up an hour later, I grab my phone and search for the local community college's website. There's nothing wrong with community college. It's cheap. I could live at home and save money. I could keep my job at the orthodontist's and maybe pick up something else—work at the thrift shop or Arby's or something. I don't know.

I don't even have the energy to turn on my Sad Songs playlist.

By the time I drag myself out of bed, the coffee Mom brewed

has gone cold. I grab my cheeriest mug—a smiling pig whose tail is the handle—and pour in the cold dregs from the pot.

I'm staring at a blank section of eggshell-white wall when my phone vibrates. I glance at the unknown number on the screen. Probably spam. Not Professor Gillespie apologizing for missing the show. Not Hughes calling to say they've granted an emergency extension. Just someone trying to sell me an extended warranty on a shit-bucket car I'm not allowed to drive.

I sip my stale coffee. I stare at the wall. I wonder how many times our landlord has painted the wall that same shade of not-quite-white.

After a minute, the phone rings again. Still an unknown number, but I don't remember if it's the same unknown number as last time. I try to touch decline, but—*fuck*—I've answered it.

"Hello?" a voice says. Then, a pause. Not a robot *hello*. A regular human person *hello*. "Hello?" the human says again.

"Um, hi?" I say, finally picking up the phone and trying to also sound like a human. One whose dreams have not been smashed like a cardboard box in a trash compactor.

"Hi, this is Jackson Foley," the voice says. "I'm a reporter with the *Pittsburgh Daily Pulse*." The voice is youngish, kind, and eager. "I'm looking for Lucy Myers?"

I straighten, the name jolting me awake faster than this caffeine is. Spam callers always use my deadname. "Oh, um, hello. This is she." I cringe. Who am I, a 1950s housewife?

"Hi, Lucy. I'm writing a story about your show, *The Storm*."

I choke on my coffee and pull the phone away from my mouth so he can't hear me cough. *What in the hot fudge sundae?*

"I'd been planning a piece on Gay Christmas Carol but didn't realize the show had been canceled. I decided to stay for your production, and I'm *so* glad I did. It's pretty remarkable for a high school student to produce a show like that."

"Uhhhh," I stammer. "Wow. Thanks."

"Can I get a quote about what inspired you to put on the show at the Finnegan?"

"Oh! Um, sure." *Think, think, think.* What inspired me? Desperation? Humiliation? "Ummm, well, we got kicked out of our school theater," I start to explain. There are clicking keyboard sounds on the other end—he's taking notes. "This was supposed to be our senior showcase—mine and my best friend Callie's, I mean." I hesitate, wondering if I should get into the whole school board debacle. Might as well now, I guess. "But the school board banned it because it dealt with, you know, transgender issues. So they wanted us to take all that stuff out."

"The school board did?"

"Yeah."

"Oh my god. I'm so sorry that happened."

I let out a breath I didn't know I was holding. Jackson is on my side. "Yeah, it sucked. You know, we wrote the show to be one thing, but then they wanted us to totally sanitize it and make it something different."

"I'm really impressed that two high schoolers wrote the show I saw last night. No offense to high schoolers. But it was really well done."

"Thanks. We, uh, had a lot of fun doing it." I can't help smiling, remembering the long summer days Callie and I spent chowing down on sour gummy worms and scribbling ideas back and forth in a notebook.

"So after the school board censored your play, you decided to take it elsewhere?"

If only we'd thought to be that brave. "Well, we tried to, you know, take out the good stuff. But we had to get the new version approved." How do I explain what happened next? I fucked up and didn't turn it in on time? *Let's skip over the whole Botetourt fiasco.* "And long story short, we didn't get it approved on time. It was going to be our audition for the Hughes program at Central, so we scrambled to find somewhere else to perform it."

"Ah, Hughes."

"You know it?"

"I'm on the arts and culture beat, so yeah, I run into a lot of Hughes grads."

The memory of Professor Gillespie's unclaimed ticket creeps back, but I drop-kick it out of my mind. I'm not ready to check off "Cry during a news interview" from my bucket list quite yet.

"And it just so happened that the Finnegan had an opening this weekend?" Jackson asks.

"Yeah, we got really lucky, because they still had the deposit from the Gay Christmas Carol reading." *Shit.* "Hold on, can you delete that part? That guy died, so that sounds really horrible of me to say."

Jackson chuckles. "I won't publish that, don't worry. And that guy was an asshole, for the record. But I do have a few more questions for you. Miranda is a transgender woman in your show. Just to confirm, that reflects your own identity, right?"

I'm about to answer but then hesitate. If I were talking to a normal person, of course I'd tell them yes. But this is a reporter. Who is typing words that might end up in the newspaper. A newspaper that people might read. "Um, are you going to put this in your story?"

"I won't if you don't feel safe having that information public. I totally understand if that's the case."

I think about it. I don't know anything about the *Pittsburgh Daily Sunshine,* or whatever newspaper he said. I can't remember the last time I even *read* a newspaper. "Hmm. I'm not really sure. Can I think about it?"

"Of course," he says. "I do have to get this story out by noon. Take a minute to think, and then let me know what you decide, okay? And I totally understand if you'd rather keep that information private." There's a pause before he continues. "I'm actually trans myself."

"Oh!" I choke on my coffee again, I'm so surprised.

"I came out much later in life than you, which is another reason I'm impressed by your show. I wish I could've seen it when I was your age."

"Um, thank you. Yeah, our hope was that it might empower some people to, you know, accept themselves and live their lives authentically." Wow, listen to me. I'm eloquent as fuck right now.

We exchange email addresses so he can send me a link to the piece when it's published, and I promise to text him my decision within the hour. He's going to call Callie next, and I give him Asha's phone number, too, since she's the only one awake in that house at this hour.

I run upstairs and flop onto my bed, my veins tingling with possibilities. On the one hand, telling my story could help other trans people come out. But on the other hand, am I ready to be the face of trans representation for young theater nerds in the greater Pittsburgh area?

I look up Jackson's paper, and it runs stories about all kinds of things—crimes, road closures, new businesses, community events, arts and culture. It's just a regular old newspaper. But if my name gets published here, anyone who knows me can search and find out I'm trans. The more I share my story, the harder it is to choose how and when I disclose my identity.

I need Alex's advice, but she probably just went to bed two hours ago. And even if Asha does wake up Callie, she won't really know how to advise me on the disclosure piece of the puzzle.

I rap my fingers against the desk. I obviously need more trans friends in my life for moments like this.

Ayden.

I swipe through my phone, making sure I still have his number. Our short-lived text chain blares up at me, in which I ask to meet up and then immediately blow him off. *Sigh.* I'm a wad of toilet paper.

Without pausing to think, I shoot him a message: I'm really sorry I blew you off when I was visiting campus. Rude. I was wondering if you'd still be up to chatting? I know you barely know me . . .

Ayden texts back within seconds. Hey Lucy! I've been thinking about you. I'm free now, if it's a good time.

I call him. His kind face appears on the screen, with light

shining in from a floor-to-ceiling window behind him. He's in the dining hall at a small table. I ignore my own sleepy, makeup-free face in the lower right corner.

"It's like we're meeting for breakfast after all," I say.

He laughs. "You should try the muffins." He pushes an off-white muffin toward the camera, like he's feeding me. "So—what's up?"

"Okay. So." I take a deep breath. "First, I'm really sorry for skipping out on our dinner plans last month. I, uh, got kind of swept away by this boy."

He grimaces. "Yeah, I know."

Right. Everyone on campus knows, according to Reena.

"I heard about him outing you in the campus safety office," Ayden says. "Everyone's pissed as hell. Especially me."

My shoulders relax. "Really?" When I imagined everyone at Botetourt talking about me, I pictured curiosity, gossip, and heated conversations about whether trans women belonged on campus in the first place.

"Yeah," Ayden continues, "there's a petition going around to get that security officer fired and for Ian to be banned from campus."

"*What?* Banned from campus?"

Ayden tells me that the same group that organized the protest mobilized the petitions. Plus they're lobbying the safety office to change their lost-wallet policy. "It's exactly the kind of thing we've been asking for over the past two years," Ayden explains. "If Botetourt says trans students are welcome here, they have to put their policy where their mouth is and actually do something to protect us."

"Doesn't Ian's mom *live* on campus?"

Ayden shrugs. "Sucks to suck."

I blink. "Do you think it'll work?"

Ayden sighs. "Honestly, probably not. But either way, he's banned for life from Sheep parties. The student body is totally on your side."

A shiver runs through me at the thought of being the subject of controversy at a school I only visited for a day and a half. But it also makes me feel even more connected to Botetourt. In my own little way, I helped change things.

"This weirdly connects to what I wanted to talk to you about," I say. "And to be honest, I'm calling you because I really only have one trans friend, and she's on Pacific time and sleeps like a corpse."

Ayden laughs. "I'm happy to be of service."

I quickly explain the showcase fiasco, the performance at the Finnegan last night, and the call with Jackson this morning. "And so I can't decide if I should, like, go fully public with my identity."

"Hmmm. That's a really tough decision," Ayden says thoughtfully. "What's going through your head?"

I sigh. "Part of the whole reason I wanted to check out Botetourt was for a fresh start, where people didn't already know my whole life story. I guess I wanted to kind of go stealth, and only tell people I was trans after I got to know them."

Ayden nods along as I speak. "So you're worried that if the reporter writes that you're trans, anyone will be able to find that out if they search your name."

"Exactly."

"I guess the question is: How important is it to you that your identity stays private?"

I don't know, Ayden. That's why I'm asking you. "What would you do in my shoes?"

He lets out a low whistle. "That's a toughie. But I think I'm at the point in my life where I don't want my transness to be a secret, you know? I *want* people to know."

Shame spreads over my chest like heartburn. I really erased all traces of transness from my Instagram, didn't I? To impress a boy? Neither of us says anything for a long time. But it feels good to see Ayden's supportive face on my screen.

"I am proud to be trans," I finally say. "But it's also so hard sometimes."

Ayden nods. Of course he knows.

"I just want to *exist,* you know? And for people to treat me like a normal human."

"I hear you. And you're right—it can be easier if people think you're cis."

"But it's a lot of fucking work. Worrying about my makeup and hair and outfits, and checking myself in the mirror all the time." My mind flits to Callie, who people read as a woman no matter what she's wearing or how long she's let her leg and armpit hair grow out.

Ayden keeps nodding. "I think about this a lot. I used to think my life would be great if I could just grow some hair on my chin." He strokes his beard for emphasis. "But it's weird. Every now and then, someone assumes I'm a cis man and starts talking to me about—I don't know—ball sacks and stuff." I laugh. "And even though it's flattering, it also hurts my feelings a little bit. Because they're not seeing the whole me."

Now I'm the one who can't stop nodding. "I know what you mean. I was surprised when I got to campus and I *wanted* to tell people I was trans. It's like I was trying to act in a play or something, and I had to remember all these lines." Which, ironically, is how I often felt when I was presenting as a boy. It didn't feel good then, and it didn't feel good at Botetourt.

Ayden takes a long sip from his orange mug. "The way you make it sound, it's just another way of being back in the closet."

I let his words stew in my brain for a few moments. "Closets can go fuck themselves," I finally say.

I know what I'm going to do.

AT 12:30, AN EMAIL PINGS IN FROM JACKSON with a link to the online article. I forward it to Callie right away and then read it.

Teens Defy Transphobic School District with Shakespeare Adaptation

Well, when you put it that way, we sound like badasses.

There's a picture that Jackson must have taken last night of Callie and me holding hands and bowing during curtain call. There's also one I sent of me and Callie waving trans pride flags at the Pride March last summer, our faces painted with rainbows. I smile. We're so full of joy.

I read the article, and my heart skips a beat when I see the quote I typed up for Jackson.

> "For most of my life, I've been imprisoned in various ways," says Myers, a high school senior. "By things people expect of me. By rules I have to follow, both written and unwritten. By the amount of money I have. And by my own body, which never felt like it was my own until recently. Coming out as trans was freedom, just like Miranda finds freedom by leaving Prospero's circle of control. I hope this story gives other people hope that they can find freedom, too, whether they're trapped in a closet like I was or imprisoned by other forces dictating their lives in ways that don't serve them."

Damn. I sound smart. And now it's out there.

There's a quote from Callie, too. She must have given it over the phone as she was waking up, because it's spicy.

> "Lucy is my best friend," says Callie Katz, who cowrote, codirected, and costarred in the show with Myers. "I'd do anything for her. Including giving our school board two big middle fingers by putting on this show at the Finnegan."

I smile, and a warmth spreads over my whole body. There's no taking this back. And I wouldn't want to, even if I could.

20

OUR SATURDAY-NIGHT SHOW SELLS
out by five p.m.

"Are you kidding me?" I ask Michael at the box office after he gives us the news. Callie has already applied her stage makeup, so her eyes widen in exaggerated surprise.

"Not kidding," Michael says. "The phone and the website have been blowing up." Michael wears a lime-green blazer with matching glasses and is organizing a huge tray of envelopes by last name.

Callie and I look at each other, grinning. Sure, Hughes is history. But we're putting on a *sold-out show* tonight. At a real theater! Because we were quoted in an honest-to-goddess newspaper!

And maybe best of all, we're making money on this show, not losing it. A knot finally loosens in my chest, and I relax in a way I haven't in weeks.

"I think we could fill seats for two shows tomorrow, if you're up for it," Michael says. "The matinee is nearly sold out, so we could add a seven p.m."

Back in the dressing room, I type out a text to Jackson.

> **Me:** Thank you!!! Our show sold out!!!

> **Jackson:** Glad the article helped get the word out. Break a leg tonight.

WHEN THE CURTAINS SLIDE CLOSED AT THE

end of the night, the audience erupts in applause that booms louder than our thunderstorm sound effects.

"Holy fuck, this is, like, the best show we've ever done," Callie whisper-yells into my ear.

I'm too pumped up to respond, so I just squeeze her in a rib-crushing hug.

My body floats off the stage, and Callie has to tug me like a helium balloon back out for the curtain call. The packed theater stands on its feet as Callie and I take our final bow.

I blink furiously to hold back the tears, but the dam breaks. I let them flow.

TO CELEBRATE, CALLIE AND I TAKE THE WHOLE

cast and crew down the street to our favorite ice cream shop. Sure, we talked about saving up our ticket money for college applications and whatnot. But in practice, splurging on ice cream is a lot more satisfying than entering debit card information on an online form. We just got our first standing ovation, after all.

"Ice cream's on us!" Callie announces, waving the check from Michael in the air. Everyone cheers. There are so many of us that our line trails out the door onto the sidewalk. A few folks here came from the audience, too, and they pat us on the backs and shake our hands.

"Don't wave that around," I whisper to Callie.

"What?" She laughs but slips the check into her wallet. "I already did the mobile deposit. I'll send you half, okay?"

"Half after this ice cream," I say. "I want to split that, too." I do the math in my head. There are about fifteen of us, and a single scoop is four bucks. That's sixty bucks, plus a nice tip for the two busy scoopers whose eyes rolled out of their heads when we walked in.

"I'll do the family sundae in a chocolate-dipped waffle bowl," Emma says at the register.

Scratch that. Let's say two hundred dollars, to be safe. Plus gas to pay back the drivers. The expenses are piling up more than we expected. But still, I'm not sad about it. It feels good to celebrate after so many weeks of hard work, setbacks, and barely contained rage.

Callie, Deja, and I get our ice cream last, and we find three red-cushioned seats together at the counter. I scarf down my scoop of peanut butter jelly time and try to savor the crunchy maple. Maybe I should've gotten a family sundae, too.

Callie lets out a huge sigh, swirling her hot fudge and brownie ice cream together at the bottom of her bowl. "I can't believe we put on an amazing show, but we still have zero chance of getting into Hughes."

"Did you call them?" Deja asks. She licks her double-scoop cone—bourbon cherry and chocolate trail mix.

"Yep." Callie nods. "And Mr. Walker did, too. But none of his friends there could do anything. They said it was our fault for waiting until the last minute."

The ice cream starts to curdle in my stomach. "How is it possible to feel so happy and so devastated at the same time?" I wonder aloud.

"I'm still gonna try to get into Hughes for my sophomore year," Deja says. "If I go to Central, I mean. I'm applying to some other places, too."

Even though I've braced myself for the possibility, the thought of spending an entire year at Central taking required math and writing classes feels like a huge, boring mountain I'll never be able to climb. Unless Callie is there cheering me on, I guess.

"Do you still want to go to Central?" I ask Callie. "If you can't do theater?"

She leans back, licking fudge from her spoon. "It's risky. Because what if I do those gen eds and then Hughes doesn't let me transfer in? I could be stuck majoring in something horrible, like, I don't know, pickle science."

Deja and I laugh so hard, a little ice cream squirts out of our mouths.

"You're so much of a theater nerd, you can't even think of a backup major," Deja says.

"Ooh, that's a good line for a college essay," I say.

"Have you looked at any other schools?" Deja asks. "Or, like, gone to a college fair or anything?"

Callie and I look at each other. We haven't told anyone in the cast or crew about our trip to Botetourt in case they thought that was the reason we turned in our revised script late.

"Well, we had been thinking about this one school kind of far from here," Callie says cautiously. "It's called Botetourt?"

I stare at Callie's eyes, trying to tell whether she's serious. "I thought you didn't like Botetourt," I say.

"Are you kidding me? It was awesome. The campus is beautiful, and the people were so, so nice. And I have it on good authority that there's a waffle bar."

"I've never heard of it," Deja says. "How's the theater program?"

"Small but mighty," I say.

"They have literal sword-fighting classes," Callie adds. "Central just lumps that in with stage movement."

Deja nods and takes a bite from her cone. "Sounds cool."

"It's a women's college," I blurt, laughing awkwardly. "Weird, right?"

Surprising me, Deja smiles. "Right on. Like Smith."

"See?" I give Callie a look. "Women's colleges are still a thing."

Callie waves her spoon in the air. "Okay, okay. I know that now. It just sounded culty to me at first."

"But you really liked it?" I ask Callie.

She breaks into a huge smile. "That Sheep party? It totally slapped! *Those* are my people!"

"What's the name again?" Deja asks. "Bada bada whatever?"

I show her the website on my phone. *"Bot-uh-tot,"* I pronounce for her. "Kind of rhymes with Tater Tot."

"Cool. I'll check it out."

AFTER EVERYONE ELSE CLEARS OUT, CALLIE

and I move to seats at the front window to watch for our parents. They all went to Wendy's after the show—Nikhil's request—and took their time so we could ride home together.

Callie, spinning on her stool, clears her throat. "So, speaking of gifts," she says.

"Were we?"

"In my head I was talking about the really beautiful embroidery you did of Meatball. Did I not say that out loud?"

"No, you did not." I smile. "But I'm glad you like it."

"Well. I've been trying to find a good occasion to give you this gift, and it's finally time." She unzips her backpack and pulls out a big beige envelope. "I was going to wait until after our last show tomorrow, but then I worried we might bomb and be in grumpy moods, and that maybe tonight is the pinnacle of our lives or whatever—"

"Cal." I put a hand on her shoulder.

"Sorry." Sheepishly, she slides the envelope to me. It's covered in rainbow and flower stickers, and she's written *LUCY* in big bubble letters on the front.

"I'm scared," I say, hyperaware of the nervous grin on my face.

"You should be," she teases.

I open it carefully and pull out a yellow sheet of construction paper screaming a message in big, colorful letters: NAME-CHANGE KIT.

Underneath is a small stack of official forms with STATE OF PENNSYLVANIA JUDICIAL CIRCUIT stamped on top. A name-change petition, a publication of notice form, a name-change order. Beneath that is an information form from our local newspaper about how to publish a name-change announcement—one of the more antiquated steps in the process. And finally, there's a smaller envelope. I slide my finger under the flap, my hand shaking.

It's a stack of cash.

"There's three hundred dollars there," Callie says.

I can't do anything but stare at the money as it vibrates in my hands. And before I can stop them, the tears pour out. I'm full-on sobbing in this ice cream parlor. "How?" I choke out into Callie's shoulder.

She rocks me back and forth, squeezing me. "I've been, uh, saving up for a long time," she says, shrugging.

"I can't believe this, Cal," I manage. "Thank you."

"I love you, Luce."

"Love you more, Cal."

When I lift my face from her shoulder, my soggy stage makeup has transferred itself onto her wiener dog sweatshirt. I sniff. "Sorry about that."

But she just pulls me in for a tighter hug.

"Whatever happens next year, we'll still stay best friends," she says. "Deal?"

"Deal."

NINE MONTHS LATER

I LAY OUT A BLANKET ON THE GRASS

and collapse for a much-needed break. I'm soaked in sweat after moving suitcases and boxes up two flights of creaky wooden stairs to my new dorm room. September is hotter down here than it is back home.

The sky is bright blue with just a few clouds. But my favorite thing about the scene is the way the mountains wrap the sky in a big hug. It makes me feel warm and protected.

"I can see why you fell in love with it," Mom says, sitting down beside me and unscrewing the cap of her water bottle.

"You like it?" I lay my head on her lap and let her pet my sweaty hair. I won't get a moment like this again until at least Thanksgiving break.

"The mountains are beautiful. And the campus is stunning."

I sigh. "I'm going to miss you."

"Good," she says brightly, and kisses me on the forehead. "That means you love me."

"Are you sure you're not worried about me being so far away?" *If you get sick again,* she knows I'm saying.

"You can't let what my body does hold you back from what *you* need to do. Okay?" Mom says.

I squeeze her hand and smile.

"Aaahhh," Dad groans, walking across the quad and collapsing onto the blanket. "That's the last of it, right?"

"Sorry, there's still my lead pipe collection," I joke. "Just five boxes, though." The dorm buildings are historic and beautiful, but it's kind of ridiculous that they don't have elevators.

Dad presses his hands to his chest. "Sorry, I think I'm having a heart attack." He closes his eyes and sticks his tongue out, playing dead.

Both my parents are in great moods. Dad's even carrying around the trans pride flag keychain I got him.

I think they're happy that I'm happy. Plus all the scholarship money helps. It turns out that being censored by your school board, giving a newspaper interview about your oppression, and helping to change a college's policy before you've even enrolled looks *amazing* in a scholarship essay. In the end, Botetourt gave me the most generous package they have. Alex thought they might be afraid I would sue over the whole campus security thing. I probably wouldn't—sounds like a lot of work—but I won't say no to a little extra money.

My folks go to move the car, and I spread my limbs out on the blanket, soaking up the juicy blue sky.

"Hey, Lucy!" a voice shouts. I sit up, and Reena waves to me across the quad.

"Reena!" I jump up and run to her. "I'd hug you, but I'm covered in sweat."

"Air hug!" She wraps her arms around the empty space in front of her, and I do the same. "So what dorm are you in?"

"Heckler." We walk back to the blanket, and I point to the brick building on the west side of the quad. "You?"

"I'm in BAA this year!" She points in the direction of the arts dorm.

"Sweet! When's the first Sheep party?" In my head, I run through the list of wild outfits I could put on. I've got a sequined romper I've been dying to wear.

"Probably this weekend." Her voice gets serious for a moment. "And you know that boy is banned, right? Not from campus, technically, but *definitely* from BAA."

Memories of Ian don't sting like they used to. Now the night of being outed reminds me of how Botetourt students came to my rescue and protected me, even after I left campus. But still, I'm relieved I don't have to worry about running into him. "Yeah, I know. Uh, thanks for taking my side in all of this."

"Are you kidding me? What happened was *so* not okay. I was worried you'd completely crossed Botetourt off your list."

"I did for a while," I say. "But I had a change of heart. And speaking of changes." I whip out the new driver's license that I can't stop showing every person I meet. I'm just so damn proud of it.

Reena's face lights up. "You got your name changed?" She examines the card. The photo is recent, and I look fly as fuck, if I do say so myself. "Lucy Calliope Myers," she reads. "I didn't know that was your middle name. It's beautiful."

"I picked it kind of recently," I say.

"Calliope. Wait. Did you choose it because of—"

"Callie, yeah," I say shyly. A fitting tribute to my best friend. As soon as I thought of the name, I knew it was the perfect fit. Callie tried to talk me out of it, in case we get in a fight one day and hate each other for the rest of our lives. But I'd already set my heart on it. Plus, no matter what happens in the future, she's still the most important person in my story of becoming who I am.

Reena joins me on the picnic blanket, where I've laid out a delicious feast of marshmallow-belly frogs and sharp cheddar cheese left over from the drive. She runs her finger over the pins I've attached to my tote bag. *Trans Pride, She/Her, Trans Lives Matter,* and my new favorite, *Y'all Means All.* "I love these," she says.

I've gotten tons of compliments on them already, and I haven't even been here a full day. Now that people know I'm trans, support is pouring out from every nook and cranny of campus.

Across the quad, I spot another familiar face. Hummingbird. But what was their real name? Oh, yeah. "Avalon!" I shout, and wave to them.

"Holy shit, Lucy!" They do an airy run toward us and tumble onto the blanket. "So good to see you!" they say, giving me a fist bump.

"You too." I barely know Avalon, but I feel oddly close to them. It's thanks to them that Callie and I were able to put on our show at the Finnegan at all.

"So, are you trying out for the fall show?" they ask, pulling a crumpled half-page flyer from their pocket and flattening it on the blanket.

The Orphaned Oligarch, it reads. Auditions are next week. "Of course!" I take a picture of it with my phone so I can remember the dates.

Avalon bites the head off a candy frog, somehow seductively. "It's my senior year, and I'm suddenly realizing I want to do *everything,*" they say. "Word of advice: join all the clubs you want to early, because four years flies by like a fart in the wind."

And suddenly, a wave of nostalgia hits me, for a college experience I haven't even had yet. I'm ridiculous. "I will," I assure them. "Starting with theater."

Avalon looks around. "So, uh, where's—"

"Lucy!" My name, yelled with exuberance, echoes across the quad. Standing at the door to our new dorm building is Callie, her cheeks red with heat and exertion.

"Callie!" I shout back, matching her tone. We do a slow-motion run toward each other and spin around in a dramatic hug, even though we just saw each other fifteen minutes ago. "Are you almost done?" She stayed in the room to finish the photo wall above her bed, which features pictures of Meatball arranged into the shape of his head.

"Almost. I need to print out a few more so I can finish the tongue." She sits down on the blanket, waving to Reena and, a little shyly, to Avalon. "But guess what."

I hand her a water bottle, which she chugs. "Um, you invented dog teleportation?"

Callie shakes her head. "No, but close."

"Umm, Meatball got a job as a dog actor?"

"No. That life would be too hard on him." She shakes her head, as if she's spent a lot of time considering this.

"Okay, I give up," I say.

Callie lights up. "Asha is getting us a *waffle iron.* For the room!"

I burst out laughing. "Oh!"

"What?" Callie protests. "It's a dorm-warming present!"

"But how is that at all close to dog teleportation?"

She rolls her eyes. "Um, because it's amazing beyond my wildest dreams? Duh!"

I smile. This whole reality is kind of amazing beyond my wildest dreams. Even though it looks so different from how we dreamed it.

"Wait till Deja hears," Callie says. "She'll want to come over, like, all the time." Deja applied to seven schools but ended up getting the best financial aid package from Botetourt. She's unpacking her stuff a few rooms down from ours.

Reena and Avalon both pull out their phones as they vibrate in unison.

"Oh!" Reena says. "I was wrong. First Sheep party is *tonight.*"

"Fuck yeah," Avalon says. "I haven't had a good party all summer."

Callie and I grin at each other. We're tired from driving and carrying in all our stuff. But we're gonna tear up the dance floor tonight. *Together,* this time.

AUTHORS' NOTES

Teghan

Growing up, I was always uncomfortable with my name, scared of puberty, and unable to relate to my peers. I had very little exposure to queer voices. *Gay* was just an insult to hurl. *Transgender* was not a term I learned until I was already desperately trying to escape a body I despised. I was thirteen, hating puberty but not really understanding why. As soon as I heard the word *transgender,* I knew it fit me perfectly. This small bit of knowledge unlocked a world of possibilities for me in an instant. Unfortunately, I learned this term from a TV show with very vulgar jokes that made the trans character into a punch line. Even if I had not picked up on the hatred, the reactions of others watching with me made it clear. Trans women were something to be despised. They were something deceptive that could not be loved. These stigmas stayed with me for far too long.

I didn't accept myself until I got to see true trans joy and hear trans stories from trans people. I needed those examples to discover my own trans joy, to finally come out to my loved ones at age nineteen, to live authentically. I want *Lucy, Uncensored* to be the story that helps a young queer person find their truth or lets older queer people heal their inner child. As they grow up, all kids should have access to stories of queer joy.

Writing *Lucy, Uncensored* with Mel was really my way of coping with the years I lost: both the years trapped in stigma and the years I spent in prison, from where I wrote my chapters. In prison, I had a lot of time to reflect on life, my youth, and my own time in high school and college. *Lucy, Uncensored* is my dream of what life might have been.

Mel originally suggested writing a book as a way to keep in contact. She has always been my best friend and ally. She helped me come out to our parents, has always stood up for me, and now has helped me put pen to paper to write an amazing story together.

Mel

When Teghan and I started writing *Lucy, Uncensored,* we never expected it to become a published book. I just needed a way to connect with my best friend during her five and a half years behind bars. Phone calls were fifteen minutes long. In-person visits were two hours, with two allotted hugs at the start and end. (We had to open our mouths for the corrections officer after each hug, to make sure we hadn't spit-swapped any contraband.) I wasn't even allowed to mail birthday cards—only letters on plain notebook paper.

Co-writing was a way for us to spend time together by living vicariously through Lucy and Callie. Teghan would handwrite a chapter on notebook paper and mail it to me in a prison-issue envelope. I would type up her chapter in Google Docs, then write my own chapter and send it via the clunky prison email system. Sometimes Teghan would get parts one and three of my email within an hour, but part two wouldn't arrive until weeks later.

Those letters included much more than scenes from *Lucy, Uncensored*. For example, after Teghan wrote about Lucy painting her nails for the first time (which didn't end up in the novel), she added a note about her own experience doing the same thing in high school, and people calling her gay slurs because of it. I'd never heard this story, in part because I was in college two states away at the time (a women's college that bears some similarities to Botetourt). And I found myself opening up, too. I wrote a chapter about Callie messing up as an ally, and I told Teghan how guilty I felt about times when I wish I'd done better at confronting transphobia. We were finally connecting with each other in a way we never had before, even with a barbed wire fence between us.

I'm over-the-moon proud of my sister, and I'm honored that she trusted me to craft this important story with her. I hope we write another book together one day—this time from the comfort of our homes, with our respective cats snoozing in our laps, and no limit on hugs when we spend time together.

ACKNOWLEDGMENTS

Big thank-you to Mel, who basically taught me how to write a novel and supported me through every step of our journey. Also to our parents, who have helped me in more ways than I can count. Thanks to my partner, Jay, for being my personal hype guy. And also to coffee, for giving me the energy to write.

In prison, I was lucky enough to take a creative writing course taught by Professor Valerie Sayers, who helped me see myself as an author who could become published. Thank you, Professor.

—Teghan

Thanks, of course, to my amazing sister Teghan for going on this writing journey with me. Thanks to my wonderful parents for never pressuring me to go into a practical career. And to my beloved Eddie for your unending love, support, and encouragement (oh, and health insurance).

Thanks to my writing critique groups for reading *Lucy, Uncensored* chapter by chapter for years. First, the Flesh Friends (that name is a long story): Zak Shea, Alys Brooks, Gideon C. Elliott, Charles Payne, Becca Cooper, Sophie Zucker, Veronica KW Rourke, Dave Nelson, and Elliott Puckette. Next, my kid lit writing group: Amanda Coppedge Bosky, Judy Dodge Cummings, Amy

Laundrie, Gayle Rosengren, Kat Abbott, and Cindy Schumerth. Plus, Jane Kelley, Deb Buschman, and Bridget Birdsall for your feedback at our 2022 editor retreat.

—Mel

Thanks to our agent, Tracey Adams. We're so lucky to have you in our corner.

A big cheer for Venessa Kelley for bringing Lucy, Callie, Meatball, and Queen Elizardbeth to life on our beautiful cover.

A huge pile of gratitude to our editor, Marisa, who believed in our book and wrote the most beautiful, self-esteem-boosting editorial letter to ever grace our inboxes. And so many thanks to the whole team at Knopf who helped design, copyedit, and produce this book.

Thanks most of all to our readers. We love you!

—Teghan and Mel